Alfred Thomas Story

James Holmes and John Varley

Alfred Thomas Story

James Holmes and John Varley

ISBN/EAN: 9783337399160

Printed in Europe, USA, Canada, Australia, Japan

Cover: Foto ©Raphael Reischuk / pixelio.de

More available books at **www.hansebooks.com**

JAMES HOLMES

AND

JOHN VARLEY

BY

ALFRED T. STORY

AUTHOR OF THE 'LIFE OF JOHN LINNELL'

LONDON

RICHARD BENTLEY AND SON

Publishers in Ordinary to Her Majesty the Queen

1894

TO

MR. GEORGE AUGUSTUS HOLMES

THIS BOOK

IS RESPECTFULLY DEDICATED

CONTENTS

JAMES HOLMES

CHAPTER VII

CHAPTER XVII

CHAPTER XVIII

JOHN VARLEY

CHAPTER I

CHAPTER II

CHAPTER III

CHAPTER IV

CHAPTER V

CHAPTER VI

CHAPTER VII

CHAPTER VIII

CHAPTER IX

JAMES HOLMES

ARTIST AND COURTIER (of George IV)

CHAPTER I

In the following pages I have endeavoured to reproduce, in as faithful a manner as possible, the life and surroundings of a man who cut a considerable figure in his time, not on account merely of his/ art, but by reason of the society into which he was thrown, and the many famous and otherwise distinguished men and women whom he met. As regards himself, perhaps the most noteworthy circumstance was the genial *bonhomie* which caused his society to be courted on every hand, and made him everywhere a welcome and honoured guest. His appears to have been one of those frank and buoyant natures that throw off care and radiate the sunshine of a kindly heart wherever they go. Although born in a humble sphere of life, and compelled to climb an arduous and uphill path to competence and such fame as he acquired, yet, while still a young man, he was a favoured guest at

Court, the intimate friend of the greatest poet of his time, and the chosen companion of many others who played important parts in the social and political life of their day.

It is the *milieu* in which his life was cast that makes the reminiscences of James Holmes chiefly valuable to-day. By saying this, I do not wish in any sense to depreciate the subject of my biography, nor by any means to belittle his work. But the story of a man the incidents of whose life relate chiefly to the beginning, finish, and sale (if he have such luck) of his pictures, does not present much of interest to the biographer or the public, beyond the brief record of his struggle and his achievement. It is different, however, when his studio is, as it were, an ante-chamber to the saloons of the great, and we behold pass through it—and as they move across the stage get a glimpse of—the figures of men and women whose every action is of interest to us to-day. And even in the case of those who may not in the highest sense be regarded as historical personages, we cannot be altogether indifferent, for they too had their respective places and parts, and lent colour and life to the passing show.

It is these considerations that have induced me to put together this life and these reminiscences. They enable us in a way to realise the life of our fathers' and grandfathers' days, and show us in what our times are different from theirs, and in what respects we have improved, and in what perhaps retrograded. Sometimes it will seem hard to bring ourselves to believe that little more than half a century divides us from scenes which are herein described, while in other instances hardly so many as fifty years have elapsed since the occurrence of events that would have seemed more in place amongst the records of the Dark Ages.

I ought, perhaps, to say that in the compilation of the following pages I have been greatly indebted to the artist's two surviving sons, Edward[1] and George A. Holmes, but particularly to the latter, who, when letters and other documents did not serve, had recourse to a very long and retentive memory, which recalled persons and scenes with a vividness and point that seemed to suggest something of yesterday's occurrence rather than of years and years ago.

---

[1] Since writing the above Mr. Edward Holmes has passed away. He was one of the most modest and retiring of men, and gifted beyond common as a portrait and landscape painter. His delight was in landscape; and some of his works won the admiration of those best able to judge of the quality of such art. But he was one of those who "never had a chance," as he complained shortly before his death. The chance did not come to him, and he was not able to take it sword in hand. But it does not matter now : those who knew him best will ever remember him as the kindly soul who loved the quiet chimney corner and a wet day.

CHAPTER II

EARLY CAREER

JAMES HOLMES was born in the year 1777. His
father was a dealer in diamonds and precious stones,
and lived in Clerkenwell, which is still a district
noted for its manufacturers and dealers in that line
of business; and one of the child's earliest recollections was of playing with the bright jewels, which
he handled and pushed about upon the table, regarding them as so many very bright and pretty stones,
and which, perhaps, first laid the foundation of that
love of and taste for colour which afterwards
distinguished him.

His recollections of his father, however, were
only slight, as he died when the boy was still very
young, not more than seven or eight years of age
at the most.

His next strongest and earliest remembrance
was of being at school, where he was constantly
making drawings of what he saw about him in-

stead of learning the lessons that were set him. He was often taken to task for neglecting his proper studies ; but finally the good-natured and —as we must account him—wise schoolmaster, perceiving that a gift for drawing was his ruling passion, gave him a book of *Æsop's Fables*, and set him to making careful drawings after the wood-cuts. Many of these he copied with great spirit, and they were admiringly preserved by the school-master, who once at least encouraged the young artist with some trifling present. This may be said to have been his first commission.

His mother, noting this talent for drawing, and following the advice of friends who were anxiously consulted on the subject, decided to make an engraver of him. Accordingly he was apprenticed to Meadows, the well-known engraver, and with him he remained until he was twenty-one.

Meanwhile many influences were being brought to bear to develop the boy's genius and mould his character. First and foremost amongst these must be reckoned the example, and to some extent the training, of an educated Frenchman.

Shortly after the father's death occurred the outbreak of the French Revolution, followed by the gruesome years of the Reign of Terror, which compelled so many to flee to this country for safety.

Among these was a certain Abbé de la Touzé, who—probably through the recommendation of some one connected with the church Mrs. Holmes attended, she being a Catholic—became an inmate of her house, and so remained during a considerable portion of young Holmes's boyhood.

From the venerable Abbé he learned French, a language which he always spoke and read with great ease and fluency. One imagines also that he may have imbibed from him some of the gaiety of heart and suavity and courtliness of manners for which in after years he was distinguished, and which served him to such good purpose all through life. In later days he always spoke of the Abbé as being of a most kindly and considerate disposition, never speaking crossly to him or chiding him, even though he had been rude or played some impish trick upon him, but always addressing him gently, and, if in reproof for any naughtiness, with a winning kindliness of disposition. The influence of such a nature upon a mind like Holmes's can hardly be overestimated; it was a liberal education in itself.

The youth's progress as an engraver was so rapid under Meadows' excellent tuition that the entire management of the plates was ere long placed in his hands ; and it is worthy of note that Richard Westall's "Storm in Harvest" and Sir Thomas

Lawrence's portrait of the Duke of Leeds were almost wholly engraved by him. In 1800, that is, when about twenty-three years, of age, he engraved in stipple the portrait of Thomas Clio Rickman, after Hazlitt, which proved to be a work of great merit.

Heaphy, the figure painter, and one of the early members of the Old Water Colour Society, was a fellow-apprentice under Meadows, and he and Holmes in consequence became fast friends. Woolnoth, the painter, was also a fellow-apprentice.

Another man with whom the young engraver became intimately acquainted during these years was William Westall, who, together with his brother Richard above mentioned, became his life-long friend.

Encouraged probably by these men, Holmes had during his apprenticeship devoted much time to drawing in water colours, with the result that, by the time he was twenty-one, he had become so proficient that he decided henceforth to relinquish engraving for the pursuit of the more entrancing art. The decision was no doubt quickened by the encouragement he received and the stimulus he obtained at the Academy Schools, in which he studied for some time under Hinton, who, on seeing his drawing, passed him at once into the life class. Meadows was so annoyed at his abandoning engraving that he vowed he would never let another apprentice of his join the Academy Schools, as, said he, it always finished by making painters of them.

Holmes had from his youth exhibited a marked talent for music, and had, concurrently with his studies in art, given sufficient attention to the flute to become an expert performer on that instrument. So much ability, indeed, did he show in this line that Mr. Novello, later the founder of the well-known publishing firm of that name, and the father of Clara Novello,[1] whose acquaintance he had made, advised him to give up art and devote himself to music as a' profession, promising him that he would make more out of it. This, however, he refused to do, much to Novello's chagrin. Novello had, indeed, gone so far as to recommend him to the principal of a large school as teacher of the flute, so highly did he esteem his playing. But the young artist was destined for better things than flute teaching; although music remained throughout a long life his chief recreation, and was the means, somewhat later, of securing him influential friends.

John Linnell once asked him why he devoted so much time to music. "Oh," said Holmes, "only because I like it." "An artist," was Linnell's reply,

---

[1] Clara Novello was accounted in her day one of the best exponents of the music of Handel on the concert stage.

"should never do anything but paint." The dictum, however, was one which Linnell disregarded in after years, giving himself much to the writing of poetry and other literary pursuits.

Whilst speaking of Holmes's devotion to music, reference may as well be made to a man with whom he was brought a great deal in contact, and from whom he learned much in regard to the flute. This was Mr. Rudall, a person of considerable means and an admirable flautist, afterwards the leading partner in the firm of Rudall and Rose (now Rudall, Rose, and Carte). This gentleman was fond of making experiments with the flute, gradually enlarging the holes of the instrument in order to improve its tone. The flute as we now know it owes much to his taste and ingenuity.

One reason for the artist's rejecting Novello's suggestion was that the sale of several small water-colour studies had led to an introduction to two maiden ladies named Jeffrey, of Worcester, by whom he was invited to go to that city and give lessons in art. He accepted the invitation and remained at Worcester for several months, making the acquaintance there of the Lechmeres, the well-known bankers of Worcester, which resulted in an almost lifelong friendship and many portrait commissions.

On his return to London he soon became one of the most popular instructors in water-colour painting; but he was now gaining so much attention through his portraits in miniature that he resolved to give up teaching. With this end in view he increased his fee from one to two guineas an hour. But even with this charge he received so many requests to continue his instructions that he used to say he felt ashamed to take the money.

Meanwhile he had become one of the " Associated Artists," a society composed of a number of men who clubbed together to rent a room in Bond Street in which to exhibit their works. He exhibited with that body first in 1808; he became a member in 1809, and continued to exhibit as one until the dissolution of the society in 1812. In all he had twenty-two works hung in the society's gallery, six of which were portraits.

Among his works in the last exhibition of the Associated Artists was the picture which first brought his name into prominence, namely, "The Doubtful Shilling." It shows the interior of a butcher's shop, the *dramatis personæ* being a woman with a child in her arms and a boy clinging to her skirts with a piece of bread in his hand, which the dog is watching. The butcher is testing the coin which constitutes the motive of the story. The picture was at that time remarkable for its realism. All the accessories, the joints of meat, the weights, the scales, and so forth, were carefully studied in detail, and separate drawings made of them before the subject as a whole was commenced. But for all that it was lacking in what we now understand as realism. Not only are all the figures disproportionately tall, but the artist has still found it impossible to free himself from the desire to get something of a classic fold in his draperies—in short, to escape from the classic convention of the period, of which we see so much in the pseudo-classicists of the time, like Cristall, Heaphy, and to some extent Glover and others.

But, these faults notwithstanding, the picture made its mark. Its fine drawing, its harmonious colouring, and perhaps more than all, the slight element of pathos suggested by the poor woman, whose dinner maybe, and that of her children, depends upon his decision, anxiously awaiting the result of the tradesman's investigation, caused it to be greatly admired. The Duchess of York, on beholding it, is said to have shed a tear ; and, what was then more to the purpose, commissioned its purchase. The intermediary in the affair was the famous Beau Brummell, between whom and Holmes the acquaintance thus formed soon ripened into an intimacy which continued until the "Beau" was finally obliged to quit England.

"The Doubtful Shilling" is a good specimen of Holmes's work. There was nothing ideal about it, but it had a strong flavour of homely humour, it was sincere, and it was natural. Reproduced afterwards in aquatint and finished by hand, it sold in considerable numbers, and was for a time extremely popular.

CHAPTER III

BEAU BRUMMELL

IT strikes one at first sight as being very odd that a man of Holmes's disposition, an artist—and one of almost feverish industry—could have found any point of contact or of sympathy with an individual of Brummell's known character and antecedents. But the surprise vanishes when we fully appreciate the sort of person Holmes was. He seems to have been a man as nearly without prejudices as it is possible for a human being to be. He had too a keen insight into character, and probably found out for himself, as a witty Frenchman afterwards put it, that the more men differ in appearance, the more nearly they are alike at heart. In short, he was gifted with very broad sympathies and could appreciate a man for the good that was in him, and not condemn him altogether because of mere foibles and weaknesses. Then it must be borne in mind that Beau Brummell was a man of genius in his way. He could not have become the arbiter of fashion that he was for long years unless he had been possessed of an exquisite taste in dress, and also in manners, as regards externals. That he was all this, the devout flattery of imitation which was accorded him on all sides sufficiently proves. But in addition to this he was a man of wit, was gifted with a fine sense of humour, and over and above all, he had a nice taste for art, and could draw and paint with more than common ability. Captain Jesse, his biographer, states that he not only "drew well," but that he ".was not ignorant of music, and his voice 'was agreeable in singing as well as in speaking ; he also wrote *vers de société*—one of the accomplishments in vogue in his day—with facility." Jesse adds that "his dancing was perfect." Holmes spoke of him as also possessing a fine vein for caricature.

In short, the artist found in Brummell a man of exceptional abilities, who, had the fates been propitious, might almost have become anything, but who was spoiled by the shallowness and fripperies of his time. Everybody in what is called the higher walks of life was devoted to the worst banalities of fashion and frivolity ; they seemed to regard nothing as serious ; and here was a man as it were tossed to the surface of society, who in his person pointed the moral of their lives, and who fluttered through society like a gay, painted butterfly, the object of admiration and envy, content to amuse and be amused, until the hard, stern, inevitable seriousness of life struck him to the core, and he was left, as all such as he in the end are, alone and in person to face the inexorable facts.

Holmes saw all this—saw his weakness and his folly, and yet found something to like and to pity in the man. He certainly had an abundant pity for him in the misery of his later days. But when they first met the shadow over his path was but a hand in breadth, and Brummell's natural gaiety was hardly the least overclouded.

I have already[1] told the story of the artist's calling on the Beau at three o'clock in the afternoon and finding him at breakfast, of which he invited his friend to partake with him. Thanking him, Holmes replied that he had already dined. "Oh, have you?" exclaimed Brummell. "What an early bird you must be! Why, this is my break of day."

It is a curious fact that amongst the anecdotes which Holmes used to relate of Brummell, was one to the effect that the dandy was wont to justify his late hour of rising by saying that he preferred not to get up until the morning was well aired. Can it

[1] *Life of John Linnell*, Bentley and Son.

be that this well-known witticism of Charles Lamb was an unconscious plagiarism of the Beau ? [1]

The artist had many anecdotes showing his friend's ready wit and droll humour. One was as follows : A young gentleman once called upon him with an introduction, and said that, as he was just beginning life, he had ventured to call upon him, thinking he would be able to give him wise and valuable advice. He explained that he had inherited a little money, that he had squandered some of it, besides getting into debt, and that he would like to know what was the best to do with the rest of it. "My advice to you," said Brummell, "is, don't go and muddle it away by paying your debts."

He did not always act up to his own precepts, however. Towards the close of his career he was indebted to Holmes in the sum of seventy guineas. Being one day with Brummell, the artist mentioned the circumstance, without the least thought of pressing the matter, and without any idea of ever receiving the amount. " I suppose you would consider that a debt of honour ?" remarked the Beau. "Yes, I think so," replied Holmes. "Then I will give you a cheque," said the other, adding, after a short

---

[1] When told that the joke was in the *Essays of Elia*, both the Holmes brothers were astonished, and said they had often heard their father give it as a saying of Brummell's.

pause, "but I fear it is of no value. I have already given several cheques, and there is not much left to pay with. However, take a hackney carriage and get to the bank as quickly as you can, and you may be all right." Holmes took his advice, and somewhat to his surprise the cheque was cashed.

Another humorous story of Brummell is perhaps old, though I do not remember to have met with it anywhere in print. He was walking out one day when a poor boy asked him for a halfpenny to buy something to eat. "A halfpenny?" queried Brummell, "A halfpenny? I have heard of the coin, my lad, but I never saw one. But here is a sixpence; perhaps that will do as well."

Another characteristic witticism of his was this. A coolness had arisen between him and a friend, and an acquaintance of the two tried to discover the cause of the breach and to heal it. "It is impossible," said Brummell. "How can I have a man for my friend who calls for two servings of soup?"

The story of his not eating vegetables is perhaps pretty generally known. Holmes, however, gave it somewhat differently from the ordinary version. According to him, Brummell was asked by a lady at table if he had never eaten vegetables. "Oh yes, oh yes, my dear madam," he replied; "I once ate a whole pea."

Most people have heard of his superstition, and how he attributed his final misfortune and ruin to the accidental loss of a sixpence with a hole in it which he had carried for years, and at last gave to a hackney coachman in mistake. He advertised for it, but though twenty needy persons came with "lucky" sixpences for his inspection, none of them proved to be his own. "If I could only recover it, I know all my luck would return," he once said when deploring its loss.

On one occasion, when on his way to Watier's— a club noted for its gambling—he suddenly recollected that he had not his lucky coin with him, and he drove back to Chesterfield Street, where he then lived, to get it.

After his break with the Regent he used to be much at Oaklands, the seat of the Duke of York, where he was always given the warmest of welcomes by the Duchess, who remained to the end his sincere friend. Holmes was once at Oaklands when Brummell was there—perhaps taken by him. Someone asked the Beau what was the real cause of the coldness between him and the Prince. "Oh, a very small affair," replied Brummell with a smile. "Lady —— preferred me to him."

When walking one day in the country in the neighbourhood of Oaklands with other guests, the conversation turned on the fragrance of the hay and what not, and he was asked if he did not admire the sweet smells of the country. "Greatly," replied Brummell, "all except that of the country folk. That is the one drawback to the country." He used to say the country people would be admirable if they would only wash more. He himself was noted for his exquisite cleanliness.

Apropos of his gift as a portrait-painter, a well-known lounger about town, named Ball Hughes—sometimes called "The Golden Ball"—once remarked to Holmes, when Brummell was known to be on his last legs, "I hear it is all up with Brummell." The artist replied that he feared it was. "I am told he paints very well," continued the man of fashion. "He is very clever at it," said Holmes. "He had best take to painting then," replied Hughes; "it would be better than doing nothing." "Anything would be better than idling about town as some do," Holmes acquiesced, with a sly dig at the fashionable idler.

As his difficulties increased and became more and more known, Brummell was gradually dropped and given the cold shoulder by his aristocratic acquaintances. But the cut that hurt him most of all was the one given to him at Cassiobury, the seat of the Earl of Essex, near Watford. Here he had always been well received and treated with exceptional kindness. But the last time he went he remained no more than an hour or two, and never forgot the reception he had.

Holmes, who knew that he had gone out of town, was surprised to meet him near his residence (which was in Chapel Street, Mayfair), and exclaimed, "What, back again so soon? But I am glad to see you."

Brummell replied sadly, "I have just returned from Cassiobury."

Holmes observed that his stay must have been unusually short; but the Beau, hardly noticing the remark, went on to say—

"You know that picture I painted and gave to the countess?"

Holmes said he did. It was a miniature of her ladyship on ivory.

"I told you how they honoured it by having it mounted on a small screen in the drawing-room, so that it was seen by everybody immediately they entered."

"Yes," returned Holmes.

"Well, when I arrived there yesterday I found that the screen had been turned with its face to the fire. I felt that it was a slight—a hint that I was not wanted any more—and I came away."

Such was the way in which the poor man, once the arbiter of fashion, was cold-shouldered out of society—the society for which he had prostituted exceptional powers and talents even of a high order.

Amongst the numberless portraits of celebrities that Holmes painted during his long career was one of the Beau. It was executed for his only sister, a Mrs. Blackyers. It would be interesting to learn what has become of this portrait.

When Brummell's furniture and effects were sold by Christie in 1816 some pictures by Holmes were sold with the rest, amongst the number being one entitled "A Family Dinner Party," which fetched eighty-five guineas, probably a commission given by the Beau in his better days.

CHAPTER IV

HENRY RICHTER

WHEN in 1813 the constitution of the Old Water Colour Society was changed so as to admit painters in oil, Holmes became a member, and continued his membership until 1821, when another radical change took place and the Society went back to its old principle of water colours alone.   To the first exhibition of the Society under the new *régime* Holmes sent two pictures, " Hot Porridge " and " The Married Man," and each year, so long as he remained a member, he continued to exhibit a subject picture or two, and generally after the first year one or two portraits, sometimes more.

In the second year of his connection with the Society he removed from No. 9 Delancey Place, Camden Town, where he had lived for some years, to No. 1 Upper Titchfield Street, Fitzroy Square, the change in all probability being necessitated by his marriage, which had taken place the year previous. Next year another move was made, this time to No. 9 in the same street, and then, in 1817, to No. 9 Cirencester Place, where he remained until his removal to Wilton Street in 1828.

In 1816 amongst his exhibits in the Society's rooms were portraits of Lady Drummond and Major Wood (of the 10th Hussars). In 1817 his only portrait was of Lord Byron. Two years later he exhibited portraits of the Duchess of Argyle and the Countess of March.

Holmes had, long before this, become a recognised portrait-painter, his miniatures on ivory especially being greatly admired for the taste and beauty of colouring they displayed.

As regards colouring, it may be claimed for him that he showed a marked advance upon his predecessors. To-day this matter of colour in drawing is but as a tale that is told. But if we go back to last century and to the early years of this, and examine the drawings of the water-colourists, Paul Sandby, Cozens, and others, we shall see how pale and watery-looking they were; and it is one of Holmes's distinctions that he saw the possibility of an advance on these, and distinctly achieved this advance.

So fine, indeed, was his eye for colour that Benjamin West once, on seeing a drawing of his, asked if he had any scheme or method of colour of his own ; "for," said he, "the colour of this drawing is equal to Titian." This was great praise, and not undeserved when the strength and richness of his colouring are considered. Many of his contemporaries, and among them John Linnell, acknowledged their indebtedness to him in this respect.

The latter—Holmes's junior by fifteen years—was for a long time his near neighbour in Cirencester Place. It was here that an intimacy was begun between the two artists which lasted for some years, until, indeed, they went to live wide apart. On Linnell's going to reside in Cirencester Place in 1818, he was already beginning to be known as a portrait-painter ; but although they were competitors, Holmes, with that generosity for which he was ever distinguished, instructed the younger artist in the art for which he himself was more especially noted, namely, miniature painting. Linnell refers to this fact in an autobiography which he left behind him, wherein he says that he obtained his first hints in miniature painting on ivory from James Holmes. He also relates that all he gave in return for the instruction was two small water-colour drawings.

This, however, concerns a later period than that at which we have arrived.

During the earlier years of his artistic career, as already stated, Holmes was brought much in contact with the Westalls, and doubtless learned much from them; but an artist who exercised more influence over him in regard to his art was Henry Richter; at least there was more in common between the aims of these two than betwixt himself and any other of his contemporaries. He, in all probability, became acquainted with Richter during the time of his connection with the Associated Artists, in whose gallery in Bond Street Richter was a prolific exhibitor. Richter was one of the first "to go to nature"; he carefully took pattern of nature in everything; and if by so doing he did not become a famous painter, it was not the fault of his great exemplar.

Holmes was indebted to Richter for many useful hints—possibly, amongst others, for hints in regard to colour; for Richter, likewise, was noted for the advances his drawings showed on his predecessors in regard to colouring.

But the point on which Holmes was chiefly indebted to Richter was the careful study he was led by him to make of each part of his subject separately. When painting his "Doubtful Shilling" he, as we have seen, prepared careful drawings of the butcher's shop, and of the joints of meat, and what not, to be depicted in it, also of the draperies to be used. But in addition to this, he adopted another method of study, whereby to obtain the right effect of light, as well as the proper pose of the figures. This was to construct little models in clay or wax, to represent the figures he wished to introduce into his picture, so as to be able to arrange them and get their proper relative positions before he began to paint. He also draped the figures when necessary. He claimed that by this method the work of composition was aided, and a more natural relative position of the figures obtained.

This also was a suggestion of Richter's, who employed the method himself.

The practice is one that cannot be too strongly recommended on account of the grasp it gives a painter over his subject, which no sketches, either in colour or black and white, can possibly do. The relative distance or tone of any figure can thus be more accurately studied, and any change in composition more rapidly determined upon than by the making of fresh studies.

Holmes found the practice so useful and excellent in the results obtained that he advocated the teaching of modelling in all schools of art.

The drapery of the models he found to be best done with a very thin material, dipped in any colour requisite, and afterwards wetted with starch, and

while moist arranged in the necessary folds, which
will stiffen in drying and remain so.

Richter first suggested these methods to Holmes
when he was engaged on his "Boys going to
School," which was exhibited in the Water Colour
Society's room in Spring Gardens in 1818. He at
once adopted them, and had put the model of one of
the boys in a fighting posture, when Richter, happening to call, advised a more vigorous attitude,
and showed what he meant by extending the arm
of the boy in question. Holmes saw at once that
it was an improvement and painted his figure accordingly.

But Richter was not always equally happy in his
suggestions. His own pictures were often marred
by the violence of the attitudes in which he placed
his figures ; and Holmes seems to have followed his
example to his detriment in some of his works.

But, despite some of his mannerisms, Richter
was one of the most original of the painters of his
time, as well as one of the oddest. He showed his
originality, however, in other ways more than in
his pictures.

He took common everyday subjects for his
pictures, and many of them enjoyed an enormous
popularity. This was especially true of his "School
in an Uproar," which, besides being reproduced to

an enormous extent by engravings, was at last printed on pocket-handkerchiefs. When the picture achieved this distinction Holmes complimented the artist, and remarked, " Now your fame will be blown all over the world."

Richter exhibited his first pictures at a very early age, having two landscapes in the Academy in 1788, when he was only sixteen years old. Subsequently he exhibited chiefly with the Associated Artists in Bond Street, where his works were said to be characterised by " a strange mixture of extravagance and genius." The most popular of his works at this period appears to have been " A Brute of a Husband," which was declared by critics to be the " champion of the exhibition." The wife is represented showing the bruises the " brute " has inflicted, and the magistrates are greatly interested in the exhibition.

In 1812 Richter attempted a higher flight than he had yet taken, and exhibited a picture in oil entitled " Christ Giving Sight to the Blind," which was purchased by the trustees of the British Institution for 500 guineas.

In 1816 he exhibited a replica of the " Christ Giving Sight to the Blind." It was described as an attempt to improve upon a former picture. One or other of these was afterwards placed over the altar of Greenwich New Church, and has been twice engraved. Among other works exhibited at Spring Gardens were "Don Quixote and Mambrino's Helmet" and "Falstaff acting the King." The latter and several other of his chief works were painted for Mr. W. Chamberlayne, M.P. One of them, "The Tight Shoe," has been engraved.

Richter, however, was something more than an artist. Painting was a pursuit that occupied only part of his thoughts. There was another side to his mind, due, in all probability, to his German descent, his father having been an engraver who came over from Saxony with the Marquis of Exeter, and was introduced by him to George III. He was an ardent and faithful disciple of Emanuel Kant, and the study of abstruse and transcendental philosophy was his chief passion and engaged his attention for more than fifty years. Sometimes his abstract speculations got themselves mixed up with the practice of his art, as, for example, in a picture exhibited in Bond Street in 1810, with the suggestive title, "A Logician's Effigy."

The article on "Metaphysics" in the *Encyclopædia Londinensis* was written by Richter, who also published a small work on "Daylight" (1817). It is further styled "A Recent Discovery in the Art of Painting, with Hints on the Philosophy of the

Fine Arts, and on that of the Human Mind, as first dissected by Emanuel Kant."

In this volume the author sets forth certain theories, more especially contending that painters have failed to observe the blueness of the light which descends vertically from the sky. The argument takes the form of a dialogue between the writer and the set of ghosts of old masters whom he meets one evening in the British Gallery.

One of Richter's pet theories, arising out of these studies, was that painters hitherto had been on the wrong tack, and that pictures ought to be painted in full sunlight. He essayed to carry out his theory, especially in the "Christ Giving Sight to the Blind," which was painted on the top of the house in which he then lived in Newman Street in a blaze of sunlight. Mr. Chamberlayne, for whom the first picture was executed, joked him on the exposure of his models to such fierce sunshine, and said he was gradually roasting them alive.

With Rembrandt Richter had no patience at all. He declared that his principle was entirely wrong, and that his colours were taken from the farm-yard. "They are nothing but dung, sir!" he would exclaim.

He must have been a very amusing companion, as well as a man of great originality, not to say oddity, of thought and manners. One day when

Holmes and he were walking out together, Richter said, "Let us call and see the portraits of So-and-so," naming an artist whose works had been commended to his attention. They proceeded to the house and were ushered into the studio. The artist, not knowing either Holmes or his friend, and thinking perhaps there might be a sitter in one of them, began to extol his own works, which were all portraits of dissenting ministers in black coats or gowns and Geneva bands, and all very wooden.

"Look at this portrait, sir! Look at this portrait!" said the artist. "You can not only see its excellence, but feel it. Pray, pass your hand over it—pass your hand over it, sir. You will find it as smooth as glass—as smooth as glass, sir!"

"Truly it is," replied Holmes, doing as he was asked.

"Yes, indeed!" exclaimed the painter. "Those are portraits if you like, sir. No such portraits painted nowadays!"

On regaining the street Holmes observed to Richter with a smile, "Most interesting performances, those. Glad I have seen—and felt them."

"It appears to me," rejoined Richter in his dry sententious manner—"it appears to me as if some ingenious, or rather I would say, some *very* ingenious monkey had been at work."

For many years towards the end of his days Holmes lost sight of Richter. Happening to be walking out one day, however, when in London, he met his old friend, and they had a long chat together about old times and old friends. On parting Holmes asked Richter where he was living, and being told, said, " I shall do myself the pleasure of calling upon you, Richter, one of these days." " Well," replied the old man in his pompous manner, " if you do I will receive you."

Holmes used to recount this anecdote with a good deal of amusement. He would add : " It was just like him ; he was always as precise as an old maid, and as formal as a logician."

This was the last time they met. A few months after his lifelong friend saw the announcement of Richter's death in the papers.

CHAPTER V

I DO not claim for Mr. Holmes that he was the only artist who studied faithfully from nature at this time, but he was undoubtedly one of the advanced guard who had such a healthy influence upon art. The well-known confession of Fuseli, that "he did never look upon de nasty natur but it did put him out," touched a failing common to most of the artists of his time ; and it is to those who were not afraid to approach "de nasty natur," but went to it with sincerity, and copied it with inflexible diligence, that the art of to-day owes so much.

Holmes was one of the very few who sought nature for everything ; and his patience and care in this respect once caused Richard Westall, a man who, like Fuseli, preferred to work from his inner consciousness, and had learned by experience the faultiness of the method, to exclaim—

" Ah, Holmes, you are quite right to go to nature

for everything ; by so doing you will gain your end a great deal better and in half the time you otherwise would.   I never went to nature for anything, and I have found out my mistake."

This may account for Westall's failure in later life, when his income, from being something like three thousand a year, fell to next to nothing.   The fact is, a new generation had arisen,—a generation of artists who studied nature more, and a generation of art-lovers who were no longer satisfied with the school of pseudo-classicists.

In the early part of his career, that is, before his commissions were sufficient either in number or importance to take up his whole time, Holmes did a good deal of work for Richard Westall, who was at that time a popular favourite, and executed many large works, in which he got the younger artist to assist him.   In some cases Holmes, being an especially fine draughtsman, worked in the entire picture from the small original sketch.

Some of Westall's more popular drawings were extensively multiplied by copper-plate in what is known as aquatint, and then coloured by hand. On these too Holmes worked, particularly on the heads, being especially gifted in head-drawing.

Westall's studio was at this time in Charlotte Street, Fitzroy Square, a region especially affected by artists in those days. An incident which happened during this period of what might now be called "ghost" work greatly impressed Holmes, and he used often to narrate it in after years. Westall had one evening given him a five-pound note in payment for some work, and he had slipped it into his pocket, and gone some distance on his way home, when it suddenly occurred to him to see if he had got it safe. He felt in his pockets, and to his dismay discovered that he had lost it. Retracing his steps, and carefully examining every foot he had traversed, he had almost reached Westall's door when he espied a bit of paper on the ground, and picking it up, found it was his lost note.

The young artist was at this time living at Camden Town, then quite a country region, and of nights, in the cheerless season, not particularly safe to go to alone, the region of Tottenham Court Road and Hampstead Road in especial being infested with foot-pads. On this account he and a brother-artist, whose studio was near Fitzroy Square, but whose residence was also at Camden Town, used to accompany each other home for the sake of safety. The brother-artist in question was George Dawe, afterwards the Academician, but then a struggling beginner like himself. Like Holmes, Dawe had been brought up to the engraver's art, and like him had relinquished it when out of his apprenticeship, taking to historical painting, and then to portraiture, in which he was successful, in the monetary sense, beyond most men of his time.

Dawe had the reputation of being a terrible skinflint, and lived in a most miserable way, hardly allowing himself decent food. Once he is said to have purchased a pig's paunch for twopence and given it to his sister, with whom he lived, to cook for his supper. On another occasion he was annoyed beyond anything, and did not get over his vexation for weeks, because his sister, being unable to procure anything else, bought some mutton chops for dinner. This, to him, was an unheard-of extravagance. There may be some exaggeration in these stories, but there can be no doubt that he was of a very miserly disposition.

A more amusing anecdote of his stinginess is the following : When he was painting his picture of a " Negro overpowering a Buffalo," which obtained a premium at the British Institution in 1811, he promised the negro who served him as model that he would remember him if he sold it. The reason of this was that, being behindhand, and fearing that he should be too late for the exhibition, he worked the poor fellow night and day. The picture sold well, besides gaining the prize, and the negro, meeting Dawe one day after the event, reminded him of his promise. "Oh yes, I remember," replied Dawe ; and putting his hand into his pocket and drawing forth a coin, he said, "Here, take this ; I'm glad you reminded me." The model looked at it with a comically rueful countenance, and observed, "I hope you won't miss it, Massa Dawe." "Oh no, thank you ; you are quite welcome," replied Dawe. It was a sixpence.

Dawe went to Russia in 1819, and remained there, painting portraits for the Court, with the exception of some two or three months, to within a few weeks of his death, which occurred in London in October 1829. During his stay in Russia he amassed a fortune of something like a hundred thousand pounds ; but at the time of his decease it had been reduced to about a fourth of that amount, partly by unwise speculation, and in part, it was said, by a legacy to a Russian lady, of whom he had become enamoured. The surprising thing to those who knew him was that he should have had it in him to fall in love with any one.

But Holmes's great friend at this time was William Westall. As already stated, they had become acquainted with each other during Holmes's apprenticeship. Subsequently their intercourse was interrupted for several years, during which Westall led a most adventurous career. He joined, as draughtsman, the expedition — ill fated so far as the commander was concerned—under Captain Flinders, for the exploration and survey of the coast of Australia, sailing in the *Investigator* in 1801, and being absent nearly four years. The adventures he went through in that time would have made the fortunes of a novelist of to-day.

After nearly completing her labours the *Investigator* became unseaworthy, and it was found necessary to return with her to Port Jackson. Here the ship was pronounced incapable of repair, and Captain Flinders was given the *Porpoise*, an old Spanish prize attached to the colony, in which to return to England for a new vessel. She put to sea on August 10, 1803, in company with the East India Company's ship *Bridgewater*, commanded by Captain Palmer, and the *Cato* of London. Standing to the north on the 17th, both the *Porpoise* and the *Cato* struck on a reef, afterwards known as Wreck Reef. The *Porpoise* stuck fast, but the *Cato* rolled over and sank in deep water, her men having barely time to scramble on shore. Westall used to say that it was a miracle that many did not lose their lives, as when the catastrophe happened nearly all the men were playing cards in the forecastle.

The *Bridgewater* sailed away, abandoning them to their fate.

Leaving the greater number of the men on the reef, Captain Flinders sailed for Port Jackson for succour in one of the boats, and happily arrived there in safety.

Westall was one of those who remained on the reef, and he was wont to describe with much humour the life they lived there until the commander's return. Once a boat's crew went to the mainland to explore, and see if anything of the nature of food was to be had. A little way inland several men fell in with a family of kangaroos, and none of them having ever seen or heard of such creatures before, they were almost terrified out of their wits, and tore back to the boat, exclaiming that they had seen the devil.

Westall managed to save most of his effects from the wreck, but in the disorder which ensued he lost a small silver palette, which was a prize awarded to him for drawing by the Society of Arts, and bore his name. He valued the article very much, and was greatly annoyed at the loss of it, but all his efforts to find it were in vain. When he got back to England he applied to the Society in the hope that they might be induced to let him have another made like it; but this they refused. However, some time afterwards, going along Holborn and happening to look into a pawnbroker's window, Westall saw something so much like his lost palette that he went in and asked to be allowed to look at it. He found, to his joy, that it was the missing article, and of course straightway purchased it. It had undoubtedly been stolen by one of the sailors during the disorder consequent upon the wreck, and secreted amongst his effects till he got back to London, when he pawned it.

But this was not the strangest thing connected with this adventurous voyage. On Captain Flinders' arrival at Port Jackson, the *Rollo*, bound to China, was sent to the relief of the castaways. Two schooners accompanied her, one to take back to Port Jackson those who preferred that course, and the other, the *Cumberland*, of 29 tons, to carry Flinders to England for another vessel. On his way home the latter put in at Port Louis, Mauritius, and was taken prisoner by the French, who were then at war with England, and kept there for nearly seven years, not being released until June 1810. In the interim he had been almost forgotten. Setting to work, however, on the record of his expedition, he finished it by 1814, but was denied the satisfaction of seeing the consummation of his work in its issue to the public, as he died on the very day it was published.

One more incident connected with this expedition is worthy of record, as it rounds off the story with a sort of dramatic or poetic consistency, beloved of both reader and narrator. When the *Bridgewater* sailed away, leaving the crews of the *Porpoise* and the *Cato* to their fate, there was one man on board who charged Captain Palmer with his inhumanity, and prophesied that punishment for such misconduct must surely follow. History does not preserve the name of this man, but he was either the purser or one of the mates of the vessel. Moreover, so wroth was he at such conduct, or so convinced that the ship was accursed, that he quitted her at Calcutta. Sailing thence in due course for England, the *Bridgewater* was never more heard of, neither she nor any of her passengers or crew.

Westall sailed with the *Rollo* to China, and after an adventurous career there, returned home by way of India. He stayed some time in India, however, and met there the Duke of Wellington, then General Wellesley, who suggested his accompanying him in the campaign (his last in India) for which he was then making preparations. Westall used to regret afterwards that he did not do so; but after being away so long, he was home-sick and eager to get back.

A fellow-shipmate of Westall's in the *Investigator*

was Professor Inman, astronomer to the expedition, whose acquaintance led indirectly to one with the Rev. Richard Sedgwick, whose daughter Ann Westall subsequently married.

The Westalls were altogether a remarkable family. Besides Richard and William, there were several sisters, two of whom married brothers of the same profession as their own brothers. These were William Daniell, R.A., and Samuel Daniell, both of whom, like William Westall, were great travellers. William accompanied his uncle, Thomas Daniell, R.A., to India, where they remained many years, helping him with drawings and sketches for his grand work on "Oriental Scenery." He saw a great deal of the India of that time, and went through many hairbreadth escapes. On one occasion, on ascending a hill, he was met face to face by a hyæna. Both he and the wild beast were greatly surprised, and appeared equally at a loss for a moment or two to know what to do. Daniell saw the creature's glistening white teeth and terrible jaws, and naturally thought he was to be the beast's predestined dinner. Trembling with fear, for he was without weapon of any kind, he yet had presence of mind enough to debate for an instant whether to go down on his knees and say his prayers or to run. As it would seem, the hyæna was in a similar dilemma, and fortunately decided to run—to the unspeakable relief of the artist, who straightway took to his heels in the opposite direction.

Richard Westall, it may not be generally known, had the honour of being the teacher of the Queen, while still a child, in drawing and painting, and won the sincere admiration and esteem of both Her Majesty and the Duchess of Kent by his amiability of manners and the care and address with which he directed Her Majesty's early efforts in art.

He was a very proud man, and would not as a rule condescend to give instruction, but he consented to teach the Princess Victoria on the express condition that he should receive no pay.

Unlike his brother William, Richard never married; unlike William, too, who left a considerable fortune to be divided amongst his sons, he appears never to have saved anything, and so in his later days fell into difficulties. It is said that when the Duchess of Kent and the Princess heard of this, a message was conveyed to him in the most delicate way inquiring if he needed any help. He replied that he did not. But as his end drew near, he became troubled about a blind sister, who was dependent upon him, and whom he feared to leave unprovided for.

He therefore wrote a letter to the Duchess of

Kent, telling her of his poverty and his consequent inability to make any provision for his sister, and asking for her and the Princess's consideration on her behalf. He gave directions that the letter should be posted immediately after his death. This was done, and the Duchess received it the morning following his decease, and before the news of the event had reached the palace.

Knowing the handwriting, the Duchess exclaimed, " Oh, here is a letter from Mr. Westall," and immediately opened it to read its contents to the Princess, who was always delighted to hear from her old teacher.

Both were naturally very much surprised to learn the contents of the letter. It need hardly be added —so well is Her Majesty's sympathy and bounty in such cases known—that the dying Academician's request was nobly responded to, Miss Westall being at once granted a pension of £100 a year from Her Majesty's private purse, which she continued to receive until her death at an advanced age at Brighton, where she lived. As Westall's death occurred in December 1836, this act of generosity on Her Majesty's part took place when she was in her eighteenth year.

Another intimate artist friend of Holmes's was Luke Clennell, who, unfortunately, afterwards

became insane.　He started life as a wood-engraver,
being an apprentice of Bewick's, but subsequently
gave up that branch of art for painting.　In 1814
he received from the Earl of Bridgewater a commission for a large picture to commemorate the
banquet given to the Allied Sovereigns at the
Guildhall.　He experienced great difficulty in
getting the distinguished guests to sit for their
portraits, and in other ways suffered many worries
in the prosecution of his work.　Finally, when he
seemed in a fair way to success, his mind gave way,
and he had to be placed under restraint.　After a
short time in the Asylum, he regained his reason ;
but no sooner did he return home and set to work
again upon his unfinished picture than his malady
reappeared, and his family found him throwing his
palette and brushes at the canvas, in order "to get
the proper expression," as he said.　This was in
1817, and though he lived till 1840, he was never
again able to resume his profession.

CHAPTER VI

PORTRAITS OF BYRON

REFERENCE has already been made to the portrait
of Lord Byron exhibited by Holmes in 1817.   But
this was not the first portrait he had painted of his
lordship.   He had in 1815 executed a miniature of
the poet—just then in the heyday of his popularity—
which subsequently became famous.   Nor was this,
it is believed, the first portrait of him that he had
done.   It is known that he painted several, but the
one in question was so remarkable for its likeness
that Byron preferred it to all others.   In his own
phrase, it was "inveterate."[1]   Some years later he

---

[1] The phrase occurs in a letter to Mr. Murray, dated Ravenna, March 1821.
It runs: "I wish to propose to Holmes, the miniature painter, to come out
to me this spring.   I will pay his expenses, and any sum in reason.   I wish
him to take my daughter's picture (who is in a convent), and the Countess G.'s,
and the head of a peasant girl, which latter would make a study for Raphael.
. . . It must be Holmes: I like him because he takes such inveterate likenesses."   In another letter dated Ravenna, 16th August 1821, Byron writes:
"I regret that Holmes can't or won't come; it is rather shabby, as I was
always very civil and punctual with him.   But he is but one . . . more.   One
meets with none else among the English."

wrote the following letter to the artist *apropos* of this portrait :—

DEAR SIR—I will thank you very much to present to or obtain for the bearer a print from the miniature you drew of me in 1815. I prefer that likeness to any that has been done of me by any artist whatever. My sister, Mrs. Leigh, or the Hon. Douglass Kinnaird, will pay you the price of the engraving.— Ever yours, NOEL BYRON.

To JAMES HOLMES, Esq.

Although this is the earliest known portrait of the poet by Holmes, his sons are of opinion that he executed one as early as 1812 or 1813, at which time they were already well acquainted with each other. But whether that be so or not, it is certain that the acquaintance when once formed soon ripened into intimacy, and the artist became a trusted, if not exactly a confidential, friend of the poet. He saw much of him, and there were few of his friends that he did not meet at one time or another. Byron's circumstances and, so to speak, his inner life became so well known to him that, despite his many failings and the wild revel of his life in Italy, Holmes never ceased to regard him with the highest respect and the most sincere admiration. For his aberrations he pitied rather than blamed him, and in his treatment by English

Society he always considered him more sinned against than sinning. In his nature, side by side with the noblest aspirations, and a will the most splendid and purposeful, there was a weak nervous strain of an hysterical diathesis, that at times gave the appearance of a touch of insanity, or of "sweet bells jangled."

Thus when he was sitting for his portraits, he could seldom continue seated or be still for more than a minute or two at a time. He would be for ever moving about, now rising and going to the window, now suddenly taking up a stick and beginning to fence. When the artist remonstrated and said he could not paint while he was moving about like that, he would exclaim with a frown, "O blood and guts, do get on!" and resume his seat for a brief space.

Holmes confessed that at times he was a little afraid of him when in his most unsettled moods, and thought him half mad. But these feelings were only occasional and transient. For the poet possessed so many noble traits and altogether such generous impulses, that nobody who knew him well could help loving him. Holmes had abundant opportunities of knowing the many kindnesses he did, always performed in the most delicate manner and without the slightest taint of show or ostentation, but rather the reverse. He himself more than once had personal experience of such kindness. On one occasion he happened to mention that a certain person, whom Byron knew, had not paid for a commissioned miniature portrait. The poet asked what was the price of it, and when informed that it was thirty guineas, he at once sat down and wrote a cheque for that amount, saying the person was poor and perhaps ill able to pay it, or words to that effect.

As to the temptations thrown in his way, few knew better than Holmes how numerous and insidious they were. He was not only well acquainted with the infatuation of the notorious Lady Caroline Lamb for his lordship, but he knew the lady intimately herself. He was an eye-witness of the scene at Lady Bessborough's, when Lady Caroline drew a dagger from her bosom and made a feint of stabbing herself, and fell with much dramatic circumstance at Byron's feet. It naturally caused the wildest scandal. Nor was this the maddest of her escapades.

One morning when Holmes called on the poet at his lodgings in the Albany, he found him in a cross and despondent mood. Asking what was the matter, Byron replied that her ladyship had been again.

He knew of course that Lady Caroline was meant.

" What, again ! " exclaimed Holmes.

" Yes, again," was the savage reply.

" How did she come this time ? "

" Dressed up as a page boy," returned the poet ruefully.

Holmes could not help smiling, which caused Byron to exclaim, " It's all very well for you to laugh, but it is no laughing matter to me," at the same time breaking out into a hearty laugh himself.

" How did you get rid of her ? " asked Holmes.

" I had to send for a hackney carriage and have her driven home."

This lady, who was possessed of a singular beauty and charm, and undoubtedly exercised considerable powers of fascination over the poet, on another occasion presented herself at the door of Byron's brougham, as he was stepping into it to go home either from the theatre or from some fashionable gathering, in the character of a flower-girl. At first he was deceived by the poverty of her clothing and the hat which covered her pale golden hair, and was about to give her money in exchange for her flowers, but a mischievous twinkle in her large brown and really *spirituel* eyes revealed his somewhat impish adorer, and he at once put her in his carriage and took her home.

Whatever doubts he may occasionally have had about Byron's sanity, Holmes had none as to Lady Caroline being of unsound mind long before Lord Melbourne finally got a separation from her.

One morning he had occasion to call on her towards noon. The maid went upstairs to announce him, and he heard her ladyship inquire *sotto voce*, "Who is it?"

The maid replied, "Mr. Holmes."

"Which Mr. Holmes?"

There was another Mr. Holmes—a whipper-in of his party, or something of the sort.

"Mr. Holmes, the artist."

"Oh, show him up," said Lady Caroline.

Holmes was ushered into her bedroom, where he found her ladyship in bed, with her face covered with leeches. She said she was not well, and the doctor had ordered her the leeches.

"How terrible!" said the artist, disgusted at the sight of her face covered with the crawling creatures. "Suppose now I were to take a sketch of you just as you are."

"Oh, you must not, Mr. Holmes! Oh, you will never be so cruel! Whatever would people say if they saw me such a fright? And Byron—he would be so disgusted that he would never look at me again!"

Lady Caroline used to have a queer school of blue-stockings about her, who came to worship at the feet of the clever little lady, whom they regarded as the most wonderful bit of she-talent of the time. Amongst the number the most respectably endowed was the well-known Lady Morgan, of whom one of the squibs of the time ran—

> How delightful 'tis to meet
> Lady Morgan in the street,
>   And then to make game of her
>   In the *Examiner*,
> In an article short and sweet.

Holmes once called on Lady Caroline when a lot of these dames were drinking tea with her. He did not stay many minutes, and as he was going the witty lady said to him at the door, " They are my tabbies. What do you think of them ? " " They are better suited for tabbies than toasts," the artist replied with a smile. " More witty than kind, Mr. Holmes," was Lady Caroline's rejoinder.

The intimacy between Byron and Holmes was such that when the poet left England for the last time, he asked the painter if he would go and stay with him in Italy. Holmes objected that he was now a family man, and had to think of those dependent upon him.

" Of course—of course ! " said Byron. " But

naturally I don't want you to go for nothing. · What would you want to accompany me ? "

The artist knew that it was impossible for him to do as his lordship suggested, and so named a thousand pounds a year.

" Oh, that's quite moderate," replied Byron with a laugh.

Subsequently he several times wrote from Venice asking Holmes to join him. He wished him specially to paint the portrait of the Countess Guiccioli.

Amongst the friends of Byron with whom Holmes was specially acquainted was the Hon. Scrope B. Davies, of whom he painted a miniature portrait. He met him first at Byron's rooms, where they were accustomed to have boxing bouts together. He used also to meet Jackson, the pugilist, there.

One day, while sitting for his portrait, Scrope Davies, who was a small thin man, but extremely handy with his fists, told Holmes of an adventure he had had at one of the coal wharves on the Thames, whither he had gone on some business or other. Some of the coal-heavers and others about the wharf, seeing the dapper little gentleman got up in the most dandified manner, began to make fun of him. Davies replied, and from the bandying of words there soon came threats, and before the smart gentleman well knew where he was, he found himself confronted by a big broad-shouldered fellow, squaring up to him in lusty anticipation of soon putting him *hors de combat.* " I knew," said Davies, "that a blow from his big fist would do for me, and took my precautions accordingly. He made a lunge at me, which I warded, and then let him have one with all my might in the wind. He instantly fell all in a heap. His friends crowded round him, thinking he was dead, and I, while their attention was thus occupied, took to my heels and ran for my life."

Holmes was at Lady Richmond's when the first news of Byron's death came to hand, and he used to cite an incident which then occurred as an instance of the blind unreasoning hatred with which the poet had come to be regarded by the very society which had at one time almost prostrated itself at his feet. The intelligence caused a profound sensation. For a moment or two a deep silence fell upon the company, but it was presently broken by the imbecile voice of a youthful "My Lord," saying, " There is one who has gone to hell."

"What did you say when you heard that ? " Holmes was once asked.

"What could one say or do, except to set the

fellow down for a fool, which he was!" was his answer.

The artist always made a point of avoiding entering upon controversial questions, which was, perhaps, one reason of his popularity.

It may be as well to summarise here all that I have been able to gather respecting Holmes's portraits of Byron. As I have already stated, his sons believe that he painted four distinct portraits, one of them being as early as 1813, if not earlier. Their belief is based upon the circumstance that the artist's acquaintance with his lordship had commenced as early as that date, if not earlier, and they naturally enough suppose that it arose out of a portrait commission.

Of one of his portraits there is a proof engraving in the British Museum. It is said to be "from an original miniature in the possession of Lieut.-Colonel Leicester Stanhope, which was taken at the age of twenty-one."

To have been taken at the age of twenty-one, Holmes must have painted it in 1809.

It is not improbable that Colonel Stanhope may have made a mistake in attributing so early a date to it. According to the artist's sons, Colonel Stanhope—"Long Stanhope," as they remember him being called—gave their father several commissions for replicas of portraits of the poet. This was just after his return from Greece, "when," says Mr. George Holmes's note, "he came with his arm in a sling."

Another portrait is in the possession of Mr. Falke, and was lent by him to the Burlington Fine Arts Club in 1889. It is inscribed at the back, "Taken by James Holmes, 12th April 1816."

Of these two portraits there are several engravings. One, in stipple, by Meyer, forms the frontispiece to the *Life, Writings, Opinions, and Times of the Right Hon. George Gordon Noel Byron, Lord Byron*," 3 vols. 8vo, published by Hey, 1825, where it is described as "the last his lordship ever sat for."

Another, engraved by H. Meyer, was published by Henry Colborn in 1828; and a third, by H. T. Ryall, was published on September 1, 1835 (for Mr. Holmes), by F. G. Moor. On the same plate was a facsimile of the note to Holmes given above. It was undoubtedly of this portrait that Byron wrote to a friend from Genoa, May 19, 1823: "A painter of the name of Holmes made, I think, the best one of me in 1815 or 1816, and from this there have been some good engravings taken."

In a list of portraits of Byron given by Mr. Richard Edgcumbe in *Notes and Queries*, 6th Series,

vi. 422, is mentioned a miniature by Holmes, 1815, painted for Scrope B. Davies, Esq., belonging to Mr. Alfred Morrison, and considered by the poet's friends an excellent likeness ; also a replica belonging to Mrs. Leigh.

Mr. Falke's miniature was purchased from the painter's son and had been long in the possession of Mrs. Leigh. None of the above-mentioned prints appear to be of earlier date than Byron's letter.

Of one, if not more, of his miniatures of the poet, Holmes, according to his sons, made a number of replicas. Mr. George Holmes has one in his possession, but he is not sure whether it was made by his father, or commenced by him and finished by his son Henry, or indeed wholly by the latter.

Another portrait of the poet after Holmes appears in the *Forget-me-not* annual for 1832, in a print by W. Finden, representing " Don Juan and Haidée." His style was very popular for a time for this class of work. Amongst others I have found the following. In *The Keepsake* for 1829 there is a print of his " Country Girl," engraved by C. Heath. The *Amulet* for the same year contains a print of his " Water-Cress Girl," by H. C. Shenton. In the same annual for 1830 appears " The Gleaner," engraved by Finden. The *Literary Souvenir* for 1831 contains a print of " The Seaside Toilet "

(E. J. Portbury), and that for 1834 "The Fisher's Wife" (P. Lightfoot). The *Forget-me-not* for 1832 contains, besides the "Don Juan and Haidée," a print of "La Pensée," being a portrait of Mrs. Hamilton. The same annual for 1833 has an engraving by S. Devonport of "Count Egmont's Jewels," after Holmes. The last print of the kind that I have been able to find appears in Heath's *Book of Beauty* for 1840, being a portrait of the Hon. Mrs. George Anson, one of the celebrated beauties of the time. The engraving is by W. H. Mote.

CHAPTER VII

IT is not surprising, when we come to consider the matter closely, that Holmes not only conceived a great personal liking for Byron, as well as an unbounded admiration for his poems, but that he considered him one of the few really great men of his time. He was brought into personal contact with him soon after the publication of the *English Bards and Scotch Reviewers*, which had completely electrified society. The effect it produced was like nothing that had happened within the memory of man; and nothing similar in the realm of letters has taken place since. It is literally true to say that the appearance of the work was like a thunder-clap out of a clear sky. Society was at once astonished and delighted; it laughed and applauded; and from these it went to fêting and caressing the poet. What the people saw in this bright and stinging satire was power—that which always first strikes the popular mind. It was the spectacle of a young and courageous combatant turning upon his persecutors and utterly overwhelming and routing them.

In the case of society, that is, of his own class, there was an added joy. It had been thrown at them again and again as a reproach that they were intellectual drones, that they had never produced a man of genius, that such competency was not in them. The best that they could do in that line was a superfine dandy : when it came to the production of genius, the despised middle or lower classes only were "in the running." Hence all the best and richest fruits of civilisation had proceeded from the lower strata of society.

What wonder therefore that the classes were delighted—that they pointed with pride to this scion of the aristocracy as to one who had taken away this reproach—the reproach of intellectual barrenness! They felt that he was in a manner their salvation, that it could never again be said that they had not produced genius, and so forth.

Their pride and adulation, in consequence, knew no bounds. The poet was for a time their pet. They ran after him; women fell madly in love with him. Others besides the half-mad Lady Caroline Lamb did this. Nor is it to be wondered at.

Human nature is the same in every age, and bright intelligence, physical beauty, and the advantages of rank and fortune always tell. And here was a man with all these—with, in especial, a kind of intelligence that ever seems to the ordinarily gifted to have something of divine in it, with, beyond and above this, a personal appearance that put all manly beauty of the time into the shade.

Thus he became the idol of society, and was beset at a youthful age with every possible temptation. One need not be greatly surprised if he fell; the surprise is, that in a society so corrupt as that of the Georges, a scandalized voice should have been raised against him. But the fact is that the society that had made such a pet of him on the appearance of the first scintillating effort of his genius, soon began to perceive that there were qualities in him they had little dreamed of—powers that would carry him far, that were not to be tied down to the narrow limits of their artificial lives and their selfish views, that would, indeed, lead him to revolt against the vapid conventionality and hollow hypocrisy by which he was surrounded. Then those who had so greatly admired began to dread him, and, as is usual in such cases, what they dreaded they commenced to rend and revile. When the tide was once turned there was nothing too vile to be said against him, hardly anything too mean to be done.

Is it surprising with such a nature, in which, as Mr. Holmes perceived, there was something demonic, something so out of the common that we regard it as almost supernatural, that the poet should fly off at a tangent and say, "You give me credit for being all that is vile—you treat me as though I were—why should I not justify you?"

The fact is, Byron's greatest sin was in being too frank, too open. He did not cultivate enough the essentially British virtue of hypocrisy, of putting the white sheet over the ghastly sepulchre, as others of his profession—profiting probably from his experience—have done so effectually, to the end that the British public has taken them according to the measure of their own pages. And yet they too had their Italian period.

Let it not be supposed that I wish to palliate Byron's faults, or to besmear him with the white-wash brush. No: rather let him stand as he is—one of the brightest and most effulgent spirits of the century, denied his rightful place in our literary history because of faults that were largely those of his blood and race and of his surroundings. And yet, what does it matter though the low-trailing lights of a decadent literature and a *fainéant* criticism belittle and misesteem? Are not his record and glory written upon the literatures of Europe? Were not his poems, faulty though they be in their art, as a trumpet-blast sounding through the night of struggling freedoms? Yes, they are faulty in rhyme and rhythm, and go often enough but lamely upon their feet. But what of that, Messieurs his puny successors? The strength of an uttered word is in its power to move and to stir, not in its perfect art, which, like ripe fruit bordering upon rottenness, always touches upon the artificial. It was truly not in him to write with the consummate art you do. But did it ever occur to you to go back to his day, put yourselves in his place *in time*, and then try to measure the magnitude of his thought? That is now, and has long been, our inheritance— heirs, as we are, to all the ages and to previous men's achievements—so that we cannot with ease justly appraise its power and influence. But go to the Continent and ask those who know, those who have watched the rise and development of their peoples—ask them what were the influences that helped most to break up the state of things that existed at the beginning of the century, and to produce the new renaissance of thought and of life, and they will place you Byron—our Byron—upon a pinnacle almost side by side with Napoleon, the scourge of kings.

They will tell you that no Englishman since Shakespeare has exerted such an influence—I will not say upon European thought, but upon European sentiment; and where the movements of peoples are concerned, sentiment is often more potent than thought, that is, than thought in the abstract sense, as distinguished from the thought that is based upon sentiment.

There is hardly a continental writer of the first rank, belonging to the last generation, that has not borne witness to his influence. Goethe, speaking for Germany, says: "A character of such eminence has never existed before, and probably will never come again. The beauty of *Cain* is such as we shall not see a second time in the world. . . . Byron issues from the sea waves ever fresh. I did right to present him with that monument of love in *Helena*. I could not make use of any man as the representative of the modern poetic era except him, who is undoubtedly to be regarded as the greatest genius of our century." Again: "The English may think of him as they please; this is certain, they can show no (living) poet who is to be compared with him."

Goethe's verdict is the verdict of the entire

continental world of letters. Dr. Elze places the author of *Don Juan* and *Childe Harold* among the four greatest English poets, and traces to his inspiration some of the strongest and sweetest voices that followed him in France, in Spain, in Italy, and in Germany and Russia. Tourgenief bears testimony, in more than one of his novels, to his awakening influence in the lands of the White Tsar. Speaking for his own country, Castelar exclaims, "What does not Spain owe to Byron? From his mouth come our hopes and fears. He has baptized us with his blood. There is no one with whose being some song of his is not woven. His life is like a funeral torch over our graves." Mazzini might be quoted to the same purpose in regard to Italy.[1] So spake Stendhal, Taine, Sainte-Beuve, in France, or to a similar effect : so others all over the Continent. But all who are acquainted with the European literature of the earlier two-thirds of the century are sufficiently aware of the stamp Byron's writings have placed indelibly upon it.

And this much more must be said : that, despite his faults, despite his sins if you will, he retained to

---

[1] "At Naples, in the Romagna, whenever he saw a spark of noble life stirring, he was ready for any exertion, or danger, to blow it into flame. He stigmatised baseness, hypocrisy, and injustice, whencesoever they sprang."— *Byron and Goethe.*

the last his greatness of soul. It would have been better if we could have looked back upon him as more immaculate, as a noble example of a well-spent life; and yet, with all his errors, he might be taken as an example by many of those who are readiest to judge, who are for ever going about with uplifted hands and a "fie! fie!" upon their lips—with all their piety, whited sepulchres, who dare not be true to their professed creed and "judge not." For he was unselfish as men go; to the last he worked for his ideal; to the last, too, he preserved his reverence and devotion for all that is great and noble and best worth striving and giving one's life for; and when the condition of Greece was a European scandal, and the world looked on in apathy and indifference, he took up her cause and sacrificed his life for humanity and freedom. In that deed, the closing one of a sad but far from ignoble career, he did more for the independence of Greece than all the statesmen and all the sovereigns of Europe. And he did more, too, for the ideal for which men should strive.

In all this I am but reiterating James Holmes's oft-repeated defence of the poet whom he had known so intimately and loved so well. He could never understand the doubt that in his old age had come over men's minds as to his former friend's true greatness, and imagined that the newer generation must be composed of men of punier faith and weaker insight. However, the disparagement which, led by Carlyle, with his "screeching meat-jack" theory—fitter one for an ever-groaning dyspeptic—prevailed so long, bids fair to give place at last to a more discriminating appreciation; though there are still bleating voices raised against him who remains to-day, as he was regarded in his lifetime by those who were able to judge, one of the Titans of the century. Perhaps the close of the century may see him accorded by his countrymen that place in the realm of letters which alike his genius and its influence imperatively demand.

I may add that almost to his latest days, whenever Byron was spoken of, and his character and genius were referred to, Holmes used to quote the noble concluding stanzas of the poem written on the completion of the poet's thirty-sixth year, in vindication of his memory :—

> Awake ! (not Greece—she *is* awake !)
> Awake, my spirit !   Think through *whom*
> Thy life-blood tracks its parent lake,
> And then strike home !
>
> Tread those reviving passions down,
> Unworthy manhood !—unto thee
> Indifferent should the smile or frown
> Of beauty be.

If thou regret'st thy youth, *why live?*
    The land of honourable death
Is here :—up to the field, and give
    Away thy breath.

Seek out—less often sought than found—
    A soldier's grave, for thee the best ;
Then look around, and choose thy ground,
    And take thy rest.

CHAPTER VIII

THE LEIGH FAMILY

Through his acquaintance with Lord Byron, Holmes came to know the Hon. Mrs. Leigh, his half-sister, the innocent subject of Mrs. Beecher-Stowe's wild accusations. A lifelong friendship between him and the Leighs ensued, the two families visiting and seeing a great deal of each other.

Mrs. Leigh, through having been a maid-of-honour to Queen Charlotte, enjoyed the privilege of living in apartments in St. James's Palace. They were in the inner court. Here Holmes and his family used to visit the courtly dame and meet her sons and daughters. The younger members of the two families may be said to have grown up together, the sons especially being in constant companionship from early youth to manhood. One of the Holmes boys—indeed, the youngest, as it would appear, and the younger of the two still living [1]— had the honour

[1] As already stated, he is now the only one left.

of being the godson of Mrs. Leigh, and being named, after her and her brother, George Augustus.

Of the Leighs there were three sons and four daughters. The eldest son, George, was in the Guards; the second, Frederick, was a lieutenant in the navy, and did good service in the first Chinese war, being one of the first to land in the boats and make the attack upon the Taku Forts. He saw active service, indeed, in all parts of the world, and came out of the ordeal rather a rough specimen of the British sea-dog. In the end he married well, that is, he married a rich wife, though the union does not appear to have been a very happy one.

He was a man of a most violent temper, and must have been a very difficult person to get on with. For a long time he was on bad terms with his father, an old Peninsular veteran, so that they hardly spoke when they met. On one occasion, as the latter and a friend were walking up St. James's Street, the friend said, pointing to a gentleman on the other side of the way, " Do you see that young man over there ? " " Yes," replied Colonel Leigh, " and a fine handsome fellow he appears to be ! " " Why, it's your son Frederick," said the other. " Oh, is it ? I didn't know him," drily returned the father.

Frederick Leigh was tall and strongly built, and

possessed in his face a striking resemblance to his uncle, Lord Byron. Holmes painted a small vignette portrait of him in water colours, which, it was generally said, might have passed for a portrait of the poet.

On Frederick Leigh's marriage a reconciliation took place between him and his father, and he was invited to dine at St. James's Palace. But he came very near to creating a fresh rupture by his brusqueness and fo'c's'le style of jesting. Everything went smoothly enough until dessert, when the young man, probably more out of devilment than anything else, broke out with—

"Look here, father, I don't at all mind visiting you and eating your dinners, but for goodness' sake, when I come again, give me something better than this red ink to regale myself on." The old gentleman seemed inclined to be a little hurt, but he soon recovered his serenity, and probably resolved that the next time his son dined with him he would give him something more befitting his vitiated taste than his best port.

Frederick Leigh was at one time of the set of the Marquis of Waterford, Billy Duff, and company, so notorious for their wild escapades about town, one of their chief delights being to wrench off the knockers and bell-handles from the doors of respectable householders, and otherwise conduct themselves in the ways of the "bloods" of their time : habits which at once died out with the inauguration of the new police force by Sir Robert Peel—hence designated "Peelers."

Billy Duff was one of the most notorious of these aristocratic ruffians ; and Frederick Leigh appears to have been proud of his acquaintance. One day he took him to Holmes's house, saying, " I have brought Billy Duff to see you ; I thought you would like to know him," as though he were one of the great ones of the time—which to him he doubtless was.

It is equally noteworthy, perhaps, as a characteristic of the time, that Billy finally married a lady of wealth and title, who prided herself upon having tamed "the lion." We should have given him another name nowadays, and tamed him in a different way.

Theodore Hook was another of this wild gang. He was a great friend of Lord Kilmorey's, who, being very intimate with Holmes, used to amuse him and his sisters with his stories of the wag. On one occasion his lordship's servant came up to him before he was dressed and said—

"There's a gentleman at the door who says he has come to breakfast with you, but he has such a queer-looking man with him that I don't know whether your lordship would care to see him."

Lord Kilmorey went down and found Theodore Hook in the hall, and with him a bailiff, who of course would not let him go out of his sight.

"If you want me to breakfast with you," said Hook, "you will have to pay this fellow £17 : 10s. He has a writ on me for that amount."

"It was rather a large sum to pay for the honour of having a man to breakfast with one," said Lord Kilmorey, "but I paid it."

This additional story is told of Frederick Leigh. Meeting Mr. Holmes's eldest son James (who died comparatively young) one morning, he asked him, "Where do you think I slept last night?"

James could not guess, and queried "Where?"

"On a bench in St. James's Park," was the reply.

It was in the winter time and had snowed during the night.

Henry Leigh, the youngest of the sons, held a place in the Board of Control, an office that was done away with on the abolition of the East India Company. He married well, though his wife was poor like himself. Henry, who was the mildest and most genial of the brothers, died at the age of thirty-two, leaving a little daughter, Geraldine. His widow subsequently married a rich Indian.

One of the daughters, Georgiana, married Mr. Henry Trevanion, of Carhaes, near Falmouth. Emily, the youngest, was possessed of much talent, and learned to draw and paint, under Mr. Holmes's direction, with considerable ability. She was, as a young lady, very spirited, and exceedingly proud of her family and connections. She never married.

The other daughter, Medora, was less fortunate; she came near being the cause of a duel, and, it is thought by some who were acquainted with the facts, may have afforded to Lady Byron the nebulous groundwork upon which to build the scandalous charges which she made against Lord Byron to Mrs. Beecher-Stowe, and of which that ill-advised person made so much.

Colonel Leigh, who had been all through the Peninsular War, was a tall, stately gentleman, who had the peculiarity, much marked in those days, of wearing a long coat that reached almost to his ankles. He was generally of a taciturn disposition, but when in congenial company, and warmed to the work, he could tell some stirring and amusing episodes of his campaigning days. One story that he used to narrate concerned Colonel Dundas, who in a certain engagement had his left arm taken clean off by a cannon-ball. He was leaning over to sight a gun, when he felt what appeared to be a slight breeze pass close to his ear. Then he had a feeling as of something trickling down on to his leg, and on looking to see what was the matter, perceived that his arm had been shot away right up to the shoulder. The strange thing was that he had not felt the least twinge of pain. He was in the hospital for a time, but soon got well, and followed the campaign to its close.

Another striking anecdote told of this hero, who was a big handsome man, standing over six feet in height, is to the effect that, being in the City one day, he suddenly, as he walked along, felt a twitch at his coat. Glancing down, without stopping or betraying the least emotion, he perceived that a man had got his hand in his pocket. Quietly seizing the fellow by the wrist, he gripped him so tightly betwixt his fingers and thumb that he snapped the bone, and then coolly cast the creature away from him, taking no more notice, and walking on as though nothing had happened, though he heard the poor wretch's wail of agony as he fell by the way maimed. A strange glimpse surely into the brutality of the times!

A more pleasing story out of Colonel Leigh's budget concerned a private who, being sent to hospital for a wound that appeared likely to prove fatal, was greatly concerned lest he should die, and his grandmother, his only living relative, not know what had become of him. The Colonel promised that he would write to acquaint her with his condition. In the morning he paid the man a visit, and informed him that he had despatched a letter to his grandmother. Said the man, as it appeared, very happily, "Ah, sir, it will never reach her. She is dead. She came to my bedside in the night and told me she died shortly after I left home. But she bade me be comforted, for she said I should get better, and return to England, and live happily." He added, as he thanked the Colonel for the trouble he had taken, " It's very pleasant, sir, to know that she is not in want, and that I shall see her again some day." The proof of the accuracy of this vision afterwards came to hand in the form of a letter from the schoolmaster of the village in which the old woman had lived, saying that she was dead, and giving the date of her decease, which coincided with what the soldier had been told in his vision.

There was a touch of eccentricity about nearly all the Leighs. So much was this the case, indeed, that Holmes, who saw as much of them in their private life as perhaps anybody, was led to the conclusion that some of them were not quite right.

Mrs. Leigh, although not exactly reckless, was a bad manager and perhaps a little improvident, and was in consequence for ever needy and in debt. As it was known that a large amount would fall to her on Lady Byron's death, one day when the subject of the family finances was on the *tapis*, and Lady Byron's name was mentioned, Holmes said laughingly—

"There is nothing for it, my dear Mrs. Leigh, but to give her a tap on the head."

"Oh, Mr. Holmes, how can you say so?" sadly replied Mrs. Leigh. "She is destined to outlive me."

Which in fact she did, leaving a legacy of malignity and hate behind her.

Both of the two remaining sons of Mr. Holmes, Edward and George Augustus, were frequent visitors at St. James's Palace; and they still recall with pleasure and affectionate regard Mrs. Leigh as she appeared at that time. "She was tall and elegant of figure," Mr. George Holmes makes note, "and possessed a face which, while not of the type that would be called beautiful, nevertheless bore, as it appeared framed in her silky white hair, the stamp of a singular distinction and even of the comeliness of old age."

One of the most vivid recollections of Mr. George Holmes is of seeing Mrs. Leigh making entries in her diary, which she used to have on the table beside her, and which was written in French. · One wonders what became of that diary. Was it destroyed, or is it still in existence?[1] It is naturally a subject of regret to those who knew of its existence that its contents, in part at least, were not made public, as it might have confuted so much that has been said to the detriment of the poet and his beloved sister.

Frequently when Mrs. Leigh complained of the condition of the family finances, Holmes would advise her to write her recollections of Lord Byron. "It would make an interesting book, and would go like wildfire, and you would thus be relieved from all your pecuniary difficulties," he would say in his impetuous manner. But her answer was ever a smile and a sad shake of the head. Once she said with tearful eyes, "Ah, no! All that I know of my dear brother that is not known to everybody is of too sacred a nature to be put in a book for all the world to read."

Both Edward and George Holmes took to their father's profession, the elder at first following in his footsteps as a portrait-painter, but subsequently, when photography began to take away the occupation of painters — of the painters of miniatures

---

[1] Mr. George Holmes thinks it must be.

especially—devoting himself to landscape art; while the younger found his most natural sphere in the treatment of figure and animal subjects, of which he is a constant exhibitor at the Academy.

George Holmes began life, however, as a clerk in the firm of George Moffat and Co., tea merchants, of Fenchurch Street, a position obtained for him by the Leighs; but finding after a time that the artistic bent was too strong to be ignored, he relinquished trade for the palette and brush. Moffat, who married a daughter of Morrison (of the firm of Morrison, Dillon, and Co.), subsequently became member of Parliament for Dartmouth. When young Holmes, calling at St. James's Palace, mentioned to the one-time maid-of-honour the fact of Moffat's election, she replied, " Oh, anybody can be member of Parliament nowadays; I expect my butcher to be returned next."

One wonders what the aristocratic dame would say were she living now.

Morrison, who accumulated a fortune of four millions, ended his days miserably in the belief that he had been reduced to poverty and was obliged to have recourse to parish relief. The poor man's leading trait had become a monomania, and so fixed was the idea of his penury that the family were obliged to make an arrangement with the parish authorities whereby he was to receive a small sum weekly for his support, the amount of course being paid to them for that purpose. The millionaire went regularly every week, like a pauper, to receive his dole, and was happy to think that he was thereby saved from starvation.

In connection with what has been written about Mrs. Leigh and Lord Byron, the following letter will be of interest, as it gives the views of a contemporary respecting the poet. The writer, Catherine Hutton, was a woman of considerable note in her day. She was the daughter of William Hutton, author of the *History of Birmingham*, and herself the writer of several novels, of a *Tour of Africa*, and of much miscellaneous literature besides. She corresponded with many famous contemporaries, and left at her death, which occurred in 1846, at the age of ninety-one, between two and three thousand rare and valuable letters, a selection from which was published by her cousin, Catherine Hutton Beale, in 1891. Catherine Hutton never married, but devoted herself to the care of her father, and after his death she continued to live at Bennett's Hill, near Birmingham.

27th March 1836.

SIR—I shall be most happy to see you at your own convenience, at any time before the 11th of next month, when I hope to set out for London, or in a month after this time, when I expect I shall have returned home. But, if you have formed an idea of me from Mrs. Leigh's partiality, and what you have seen of my own letters, you will be disappointed. I owe much of Mrs. Leigh's partiality to the kindness of her own disposition, and much to my admiration of Lord Byron. As a poet, there can be but one opinion of him, except another may be formed by prejudice or envy; but, as a man, I think no one was ever so ill understood, so misrepresented, so persecuted, so unfortunate in every connexion but that with his sister. There was much good in Lord Byron that never was elicited; many of his errors were forced upon him by circumstances, and others were the consequences of the temperament which constituted the poet. I envy you for having studied his countenance. The engraving is beautiful, and I doubt not that the miniature is more so. I rejoice that it is in your custody.

As regards myself, you have to lower your imagination as much as possible before you meet an infirm old woman of four-score, who during the last year and a half has been a martyr to ill-health. A little of my former spirit may, and I believe does, remain in my letters,' but in conversation it has been subdued by time and suffering. I live alone, I admit nobody, though Sir Arthur de Capell Brooke,[1] the North Cape traveller, has been an exception, and I hope you will prove another. I never dine. My nearest approach to dinner is a *small* tray, with two *small* slices of meat (hot or cold, as it may happen), a *small* pudding, or tart, or a *little* preserved fruit, and *one* glass of wine. This I sit down to at two o'clock, and fifteen or twenty minutes take it all away. I am out from eleven to twelve o'clock every day that winds and storms permit. If you

---

[1] Sir Arthur de Capell Brooke, of Oakley Hall, Northamptonshire, was the author of several books of travel, one of them being *Travels through Sweden, Norway, and Finmark to the North Pole, in the Summer of* 1820.

will have the goodness to let me know when I may expect you, by a note put into the Birmingham post-office the evening before, the latter part of my daily avocation shall be omitted.— I am, sir, your very obliged   CATHERINE HUTTON.

To JAMES HOLMES, Esq.

I have no information as to whether Holmes paid the visit here referred to, but in all probability he did.   He had many friends in that part of the country, at Worcester, in Shropshire, etc., and spent much time there, especially in his latter years.   On one occasion, when about to make a journey to Birmingham, the following humorous incident occurred.   Meeting one day Sir Henry Peyton, a noted four-in-hand driver and sporting man, in Grosvenor Place, he informed him in the course of conversation that he was about to go to Birmingham.   "Oh, are you?" said Sir Henry. "How are you going?"   "By the new railway,"[1] Holmes replied.   "New railway! new railway!" cried the sporting man.   "'Pon my life, I'd rather walk."

[1] The London and Birmingham Railway was opened in 1838.

CHAPTER IX

HOLMES A COURTIER

OF the three pictures Holmes exhibited in 1817, one, "The Michaelmas Dinner," as it was then called, he always regarded as amongst the best of his productions. It appeared in the exhibition catalogue with the following lines from Lord Chesterfield: "He cannot hit the joint, but in his vain efforts to cut through the bone, splashes the company," and hence is said to have been suggested by that quotation; but his sons inform me that it was an exhibition of clumsiness in carving a goose on the part of Colonel Paisley, the engineer who raised the *Royal George*, which foundered in Portsmouth Harbour, that actually gave their father the idea of his picture, and that suggested the title, "The Un-skilful Carver," which it afterwards bore. It is the most elaborate and studied of his works, and may be taken as a good example of his style, and also of the kind of subjects he preferred to treat, which, belonging to a popular, sometimes, it may even be said, to a vulgar class, allied him to the Dutch more than to the Italian School.

On being shown to the Prince Regent, he at once ordered it to be bought, and it passed into the Royal Collection. It was exhibited in a loan collection in 1823, being lent for the purpose by the King. The following letter has reference to the fact :—

DEAR SIR—I have written by His Majesty's commands to Brighton to have the picture forwarded to you, which you will have the goodness to take the greatest care of, and have returned to Mr. Saunders, Pavilion, Brighton, when the exhibition is closed.—I am, dear sir, yours, CONYNGHAM.

WINDSOR, 17*th June* 1823.

In 1819 Holmes exhibited two miniatures in the Royal Academy, which were greatly admired, and brought him very prominently into public notice. The result was a considerable increase of his patronage among the upper classes. He had previously commenced to enjoy some Court patronage, and was soon in the full tide of success.

One of his earliest friends in Court circles was Princess Esterhazy, cousin of George IV, and wife of Prince Esterhazy, a notable man in his time, but chiefly famous in England for the number and value of his diamonds, and for his jewellery generally, one of Barham's most popular ballads celebrating

him in "Barney Maguire's Account of the Coronation" in the following couplet :

'Twould have made you crazy to see Esterhazy
All jools from his jasey to his di'mond boots.

Of Princess Esterhazy, the artist painted at one
time or another at least twelve or thirteen portraits.
When she wished specially to please a friend or
admirer, she could think of nothing better than the
gift of a miniature by Holmes as a souvenir. The
Princess not only appreciated his art very highly,
but admired him greatly as a man, and continued to
be on the most friendly terms with him so long as
she remained in England. On finally leaving this
country for Austria, she sent him a handsome jewel,
accompanied by the following note :—

Tuesday Morning.

Princess Esterhazy's compliments to Mr. Holmes ; she has
the pleasure to send him her little debt, and at the same time a
little souvenir which she begs him to accept, and hopes he will
wear in remembrance of her. Princess Esterhazy thinks it very
likely she may call on Mr. Holmes in the course of the day to
look at the miniature which is not quite finished.

One of the portraits of the Princess was engraved, as will be seen from the following note of
the Duchess of Richmond, dated 1831 :—

The Duchess of Richmond presents her compliments to Mr.
Holmes, and in answer to his letter, begs to inform him she will send

for the miniature, painted by Mr. Holmes, which is now at Goodwood, and as soon as she receives it, will send it to Mr. Holmes.

The Duchess is very much obliged to Mr. Holmes for the offer of the print of the Princess Esterhazy, which she will be happy to accept.

It was through the influence of Princess Esterhazy that the artist received his first invitation to Court. The earliest intimation he had that he was to be thus honoured was as follows. One morning Lady Aylmer said to him, " Mr. Holmes, you will shortly have a chance to try your fortunes at Court, or I am much mistaken. I heard the Princess Esterhazy yesterday evening speaking of you in the most flattering terms to the Prince Regent, and His Royal Highness appeared greatly interested."

A few days later he was sent for by the Prince, the immediate outcome being a commission to paint a portrait of His Royal Highness.

In all, Holmes painted four portraits of George IV, one of them being taken for the purpose of reproduction by engraving. For this the King kindly consented to sit, and it is still in the possession of the artist's sons.

He also painted a portrait of His Royal Highness the Duke of Clarence, in his uniform of Lord High Admiral; and miniature portraits of the Princess Sophia, then residing at Kensington Palace. During his visits to the palace for this purpose the artist frequently had the pleasure of meeting Madame d'Arblay, of whom he always spoke in the highest terms of praise. Her conversation, he used to say, was exceedingly interesting. Sometimes she read while he painted, and these exercises he found hardly less interesting than her talk.

The following letter refers to one of these miniatures :—

Madame d'Arblay has just been honoured with the commands of Her Royal Highness the Princess Sophia to beg of Mr. Holmes that he will be so good as to trust Her Royal Highness with the loan of her picture for this evening : she engages willingly to assure him that it shall not go out of her hands, and that it shall be returned to him to-morrow morning at an early hour.

Her R. H. begs it may be sent sealed up. The bearer is to carry it to Kensington Palace immediately.

Madame d'Arblay is to have the pleasure of witnessing the last sitting for this charming composition on Wednesday.

Monday, *1st October* 1821.

One of his portraits of George IV Holmes was working on at the time of the King's accession to the throne, and His Majesty invited him to be present at the coronation. A ticket was accordingly sent him for the ceremony at the Abbey. It admitted him, however, only to an inferior place, where he would see but little of the ceremony. He accordingly told the Marquis of Conyngham that the King had said he was to have one of the best places.

"You can't," replied the Marquis. "There are only a few, and they are all taken up by the peers and peeresses."

"All right, your lordship," rejoined the artist. "I only tell you what the King said."

"It's all very well for His Majesty to order," grumbled Conyngham, "but it can't be done."

However, Holmes got his ticket for a front seat.

During his next sitting the King asked him if he had received a ticket for the coronation.

"I have received one for the church," said Holmes.

"Oh, give him one for Westminster Hall as well," said the King, turning to Conyngham.

Thus he was enabled to see the ceremony well enough to take a pencil note of it. He afterwards made a sketch of the coronation, apparently with the intention of painting a picture of it, but it was never proceeded with.

Holmes used to describe, with a good deal of detail, the scene both in the Abbey and in Westminster Hall, with the commotion occasioned by the attempt made by the Queen to enter and take part in the ceremony.

But long before this Holmes's suavity of manners and invariable good humour, joined to his talents as an artist and as a musician, had rendered him a great favourite at Court, and he became a frequent guest at His Majesty's evening parties. Indeed, his company and conversation were so much liked by the King, that the Marquis of Conyngham once remarked that " Mr. Holmes had become the King's hobby."

On these occasions he was frequently required to display his proficiency as a performer on the flute. One evening he was called upon to play a duet with Lady Elizabeth Conyngham, and he acquitted himself so well that the King complimented him by saying, " Played with great taste and feeling, Mr. Holmes ; you are always welcome to the palace."

On another occasion His Majesty, who had a good bass voice, proposed a glee, and asked Sir Andrew Barnard and Holmes to take part with him in " Life's a Bumper." When this was finished the King proposed another and another, until quite a number were sung, His Majesty taking part in each.

At this period Holmes seems to have spent a good deal of time at Court, and naturally saw much of the inner life of the palace, of which he had many amusing anecdotes to tell.

On one occasion, when the Court was at Brighton, the artist, through an act of forgetfulness or negligence, came very near forfeiting his royal patron's friendship.   Thinking that he would not be wanted, he went to Worthing or somewhere in the neighbourhood, and stayed away for some time.   Meanwhile he was wanted by the Regent, and was sought for high and low.   Returning eventually, and learning from his landlady that he had been called for, he repaired to the palace, where he found His Royal Highness in a state of great wrath at his prolonged absence.

Holmes apologized, making some lame excuse to the effect that his landlady had not told him that he was wanted, or something of the kind.   Meanwhile the Regent walked moodily from room to room, grunting and explosive, the artist humbly following.   Finally His Royal Highness, coming to a sudden stand and confronting him, exclaimed petulantly, " What a d—d fellow you are, Holmes! But come with me, and I will tell you what I wish you to do."   So the matter blew over.

On another occasion, when they were alone together, George asked the artist what he could do for him.   Not being up to the trick of begging, Holmes replied that he was in want of nothing, he was quite content—or words to that effect.

When he came to know the Court better, and saw what a shameless system of intrigue was carried on, and how everybody about His Majesty was scheming for place or emolument, he reflected, and used to say, that had he had his wits about him, he might by a word have secured some post or office that would have proved a sinecure for life ; "perhaps even a colonelcy," he would add with a laugh, knowing as he did what went on.

He used to think that it might have been because he never sued for favours, either for himself or others, that he enjoyed so much of the King's favour. Stupid and dull as George was considered by some, to the artist-courtier he always appeared to have perspicacity enough to see what a set of fawning and self-seeking sycophants he had about him, and, in his heart of hearts, probably to despise most of them.

To what depths of meanness some of them could descend is exemplified by a little incident in connection with a cheque which the artist received for portrait commissions and the picture of "The Unskilful Carver," referred to above. The total amount was £500, £250 being for portraits. Sir Benjamin Blomfield, keeper of the Prince's Privy Purse,[1] observed that it was a "lot of money," and as the remark was couched in such a way that it seemed to convey a hint, Holmes offered him a loan of £20.

An amusing incident which the artist witnessed,

[1] Sir Benjamin Blomfield became Receiver General of the Duchy of Cornwall and Keeper of the Privy Purse in 1817. He was subsequently raised to the peerage.

and which he was fond of narrating, was the following. Sir Edmund Nagle, another of the royal household, was in the habit of falling asleep in the midst of the royal assemblies, and sleeping so soundly that nothing could wake him—"not even my performance on the flute," Holmes would say. One evening a wag, observing him in his usual condition, took off his spectacles, smeared them with wax from a candle, and then carefully replaced them on his nose. When at length Sir Edmund awoke, he could not at first make out what was the matter, that he was unable to see. But when he realised the nature of the jest that had been played upon him, he broke into a towering passion, and raged and swore about the place in the most furious manner, utterly regardless of the presence he was in and of the fact that ladies were there. Not content with this, he offered ten guineas to any one who would tell him who was the perpetrator of the joke. The offer was received with roars of laughter, in which the Prince Regent joined. This exasperated Sir Edmund still more, and with further imprecations on all present, he rushed out of the room, swearing he would never return. Of course he did not carry out his threat.

For a time Holmes was so prime a favourite with George IV that he roused some jealousy amongst the courtiers. One day some grumbling took place because the King was engaged in close conversation with him when they wanted to go out. The Marquis of Conyngham once attempted a slight trick with him, in order to lower him in the King's esteem, but fortunately without effect. It was a rule in Court etiquette that no one should enter the presence of the King unattended. It was usual therefore for the artist to be accompanied into the room where His Majesty was by the Marquis. One morning he presented himself at the time appointed for a sitting, but found no Marquis to escort him. He waited in the ante-chamber for a minute or two, and then hearing the King's and other voices within, and knowing that he was expected, he boldly opened the door and entered. The King was standing in the middle of the room, with several gentlemen about him. Holmes approached, bowed, and uncovering his canvas, began to work.

Some little time afterwards the Marquis of Conyngham entered, looking hot and flurried, and in an undertone commenced to expostulate with Holmes for not waiting in order to be properly announced. "Oh, my dear Marquis," returned Holmes, always polite and courtly, but quietly laughing in his sleeve, "I could not think of giving you the trouble to wait on me—I could not think of it."

The Marquis withdrew, smiling and courteous, but knowing that his plot had been foiled, and none the better pleased on that account. It was his plan to have made the artist keep the King waiting, and so ruffle his temper, and perhaps receive a sharp reprimand for unpunctuality.

As regards the ladies of George IV's Court, Holmes had no great idea of their beauty. He used to say they were rather a common-looking lot, and that the Princess Esterhazy easily bore off the palm both for charm of feature and grace of form. Added to this she had a fine carriage, and appeared like a veritable queen among the rest. Such at least was the artist's opinion.

CHAPTER X

ARISTOCRATIC FRIENDS AND OTHERS

THE glitter of the Court did not spoil Holmes's love for art, nor in any way detract from the mildly democratic sentiments with which he had been imbued early in life, and which in a more or less philosophical form characterized the political views of the more generous spirits of the time. His experience of Court life, indeed, rather tended to deepen those sentiments. "It would be hard to find a sphere in life," he once said, "in which men and women appeared to a worse advantage to any one capable of looking beneath the surface, and estimating the motives that actuated them. There were some bright exceptions; but the majority of those who habitually surrounded the King lived in a constant whirl of petty intrigue and calculating selfishness, unrelieved by any spark of generosity or nobility of feeling. Lady Conyngham, the King's mistress,[1] aided by her husband and daughter, lost no opportunity of despoiling him, and the others, for the most part, looked on, outwardly polite and complaisant, though secretly eaten up with spite and jealousy, and made what they could." Altogether, according to his description, it was a despicable and degrading scene.

One day, before Holmes knew the Court so well as he afterwards came to do, he happened to remark to Sir Benjamin Blomfield that the Marquis of Conyngham was a very obliging and good-natured man.

"Oh, very obliging, and exceedingly good-natured," returned the courtier with a cynical leer. " His Majesty has every proof of it."

The artist's acquaintance with the Court continued until the death of the King, and was never renewed. William IV he utterly despised, and could never be induced to appear at Court after his accession. This feeling arose partly out of his treatment of Mrs. Jordan, whom Holmes knew slightly, and whose earnings at the theatre the King, as Prince, used to wait at the stage door

---

[1] Greville in his Memoirs (vol. i. p. 27) says: " Somebody asked Lady Hertford 'if she had been aware of the king's admiration for Lady Conyngham.' She replied that 'intimately as she had known the king, and openly as he had talked to her upon every subject, he had never ventured to speak to her upon that of his mistresses.'"

on pay-nights to receive, and then to spend upon himself.

Nor did he think any the better of him when, on becoming King, he caused the now-dethroned Lady Conyngham to be despoiled of the booty, including many precious royal heirlooms, which she had wheedled out of her royal lover. Barely, indeed, was the King dead before her house was forcibly entered and the valuables therein stored, carried away, the poor woman the while being exposed to the gibes and insults of the populace.

One of the last things that took Holmes to Court was the painting of an oil portrait of the King, which His Majesty gave him the permission to take for engraving. The portrait—a very good one—is still in the possession of the artist's sons. The print was finished and published in 1828, and is referred to in the following letters by the Marquis of Conyngham :—

DEAR SIR—If you will send one of your prints carefully packed up, directed to my care, I will with pleasure submit it to His Majesty. Send the print to 105 Pall Mall and it will be forwarded.—Truly yours, CONYNGHAM.

22nd November 1828.
Private.

DEAR SIR—I return you the engraving of His Majesty, which I hope you will receive safe. As you flatter me with desiring my opinion of the engraving, I confess I think the face rather too grave-looking and the upper lip not quite flat enough, as in your original drawing.   The engraving is very good indeed.—Yours, dear sir, very truly,   CONYNGHAM.

5th December 1828.

It was about this time that the artist was introduced to Donna Maria II, Queen of Portugal, then on a visit to England, and received a large commission from her for portraits of herself.   The order was for eight or nine, but Holmes, after finishing the third or fourth, refused to do any more because Her Majesty was so atrociously ugly.   He found it much more agreeable painting portraits of English beauties, of whom, in his time, he must have done hundreds.   He used to say that there was hardly a family in the ranks of our aristocracy for whom he had not executed commissions for portraits (chiefly miniatures) at one time or another.   It was also a rather proud boast of his that few artists could have painted more royalties than he had.

Amongst other members of reigning families upon whom his brush was engaged about this time, was the Duc d'Orleans, the eldest child of Louis Philippe, who not very long afterwards was killed in Paris by the running away of his horses.   He sat to Holmes for his portrait during a brief sojourn in this country.   On his first visit to Wilton Street (whither the artist had removed in 1828) the door was opened by a pretty maid, and being struck by her good looks, the Prince addressed her with—

"*Parlez-vous français, mademoiselle?*"

"No," replied the maid with a curtsey.

"But you understood me," returned the Prince.

"Yes, but I did not speak French," was the girl's prompt reply.

This last answer so greatly amused the Prince that he related the incident to Holmes.

Another anecdote that the artist used to relate of the Duc d'Orleans is perhaps better worth repeating. One day when he was sitting his valet came out of the studio and said His Royal Highness would like a cup of tea. The beverage was duly provided, and presently the valet returned, saying that the tea was too strong, and that the Prince would like some hot water to weaken it. This was sent in. Very soon, however, the valet was back again, saying that the tea was now too hot, and that his royal master would like some cold water to cool it. But even with the addition of the cold water, the tea was not quite right, for after a minute or two more, the valet returned for the fourth time with the request that he might have a drop of cognac to correct the tea and make it to His Royal Highness's taste.

No wonder Holmes thought this a somewhat roundabout way to arrive at the cognac.

Another of the artist's acquaintances of this period was the redoubtable Count D'Orsay, of whom, at one time or another, he saw a great deal, albeit without being greatly struck with admiration for him—apart, that is, from his clothes. Holmes always had great taste in dress, and although he was simplicity itself in his own attire, he had ever an artist's eye for costume, and did not look with dislike upon the brave foppery of the Georgian dandy. But while he may have admired D'Orsay the dandy, he utterly despised D'Orsay the painter, regarding him, as did most of his artist *confrères*, as a trickster, being able to do little in the artistic line himself, and succeeding simply by having resort to the now well-known expedient of employing a "ghost." An artist named Mackie worked for him for a long time in this way. He used to be hidden behind a screen in which there was a little hole for him to peep through (unseen and unsuspected of course by the sitter) and so make his study. Meanwhile D'Orsay would be busy at his easel pretending to paint. But it was a peculiarity of his method that he would never allow anyone to watch him at work. In short, he succeeded by dash, dress, and effrontery.

He used to drive about town and go to his sitters' houses in a handsome cabriolet, accompanied by his tiger. This gaudily-dressed little creature, as may be seen in the prints of the time, stood at the back of the vehicle, and on his master's wishing to descend, would jump down from his perch and either hold the horse's head or take the reins. Or, if there was nothing more to be done, he would simply deliver his master's message or card. D'Orsay, who had the credit of being the inventor of the tiger, prided himself on having the smallest specimen of the article in town. He was so tiny that he had to make a goodly jump to reach Holmes's knocker; and it used to be a constant source of delight to the artist's children to see the Count's carriage drive up and then to watch the tiger's agile assaults upon the knocker, at which he had generally to make several jumps before achieving success.

Amongst the men of his own profession with whom Holmes associated more or less intimately at this time, was John Varley, who was one of the "characters" of the day. He had a circle of his own, which included some of the most notable men, whether in science or art, of the time, and was greatly sought after both on account of his good-nature and the queer conglomeration of "sciences" with which he was filled. But while Holmes had the highest esteem for his undoubted attainments in art, he laughed at his astrological notions and whimsical theories generally. For some time they were near neighbours. This was when Holmes was living at No. 9 Cirencester Place and Varley was in Great Titchfield Street.

Of Varley's circle was William Blake, the poet-artist, of whom Holmes saw and heard much from time to time. But while he respected and looked with some admiration upon his art, he had not the kind of temperament to care for his mystico-poetical writings. What was not perfectly clear to him was, it must be confessed, little better than rubbish. Hence he could no more understand Linnell's patronage of Blake, and what he considered the exaggerated praise of his work, than Linnell could understand his—that is, Holmes's—devotion to music. Less still could he appreciate the enthusiastic discipleship of such men as Richmond, Palmer, and Calvert, who, whenever they could, sat at Blake's feet, drank in his wisdom, and imitated his work and ways.

An amusing anecdote may be given here in illustration of the Blakeish spirit that was cultivated by these men. It has reference to Edward Calvert, and was communicated to me by Miss Linnell, of

Redstone Wood, Redhill. Calvert, who was very intimate with the family, was one day at her father's house in Porchester Terrace, Bayswater, and was describing one of his drawings, representing a landscape with sheep, a brook, and so forth, which he did in these terms. "These are God's fields," said he, in a low, solemn voice to Miss Linnell and her sisters; "this is God's brook, these are God's trees, and those are God's sheep and lambs." "Then why," asked John Linnell, who was sitting near, "then why don't you mark them with a big G?"

Whilst referring to Blake and things Blakeish, it is worth while noting the fact that the colouring of the poet-artist's later works is said to have been much improved through the influence of Holmes and Richter, both of whom were noted as amongst the first colourists of their day.

As time went on, and his hands became as full as they would hold of miniature work, Holmes did fewer and fewer subject pictures; although now and for some years to come, he was executing commissions in that line for Sir Henry Meux and others.

In 1827 he painted an important work entitled "Oimè! Santa Maria," representing a poor Italian image boy standing over his tray of broken wares in the midst of a number of unsympathetic bystanders. All the figures are broken except one, and that one Napoleon Bonaparte. This circumstance was remarked by the critics, who drew from it the inference that the artist had introduced some political feeling into the picture. The simple fact is that Holmes had the greatest admiration for the "Little Corporal," and took this way of indicating that his image, in his mind, was still unbroken. He used to say that the world hitherto had produced only two great men, and they were Napoleon and Hogarth.

Where this picture went I have not been able to discover.

CHAPTER XI

In personal appearance Holmes was, like many men of genius, comparatively short of stature and inclined to spareness of figure rather than the reverse. He was, however, very strongly built, quick of motion, and of a vivacity of temperament that often enabled him to overcome an obstacle by the mere impetuosity of his attack, where more powerful, though slower, men would have hesitated and failed. Thus once in Piccadilly he made a dash at a runaway horse which had put the occupants of the carriage behind it in great peril, and almost miraculously succeeded in stopping it. When asked if it had not occurred to him how much danger he ran, he replied that he had had no time to think of anything but the danger the occupants of the carriage were in.

He always enjoyed the best of health, which doubtless contributed in no small degree to the geniality of his disposition. Though exceedingly sprightly in conversation, and of a witty and humorous turn, he was but little given to saying sarcastic things. He could on occasion, however, very aptly turn the tables on people ; as, for instance, when at the table of a friend, he met a phrenologist, who, after pestering others with his professional observations, turned to Holmes and, unasked, began to finger his "bumps" and explain their significance.

"You seem to have most of the organs well developed, sir," he began. "Wit, comparison, imitation——"

"There is one at least that I have not got," replied the artist.

"And pray what is that?" queried the phrenologist.

"The bump of gullibility," returned Holmes.

But the most striking of his qualities was the almost perpetual good spirits that he enjoyed. Depression or dejection was known to him never for long at a time. It was this invariable serenity of temper and cheerful outlook upon the world that caused the somewhat gloomy Walpole (Lord Derby's Home Secretary) to reply to him on one occasion when he had remarked on the fineness of the weather, "Ah, it is always fine weather with you, Mr. Holmes."

This incident, however, occurred somewhat later in life, when the artist used to meet the politician at Ealing, where he lived, and where Holmes used to be a frequent guest of the Misses Perceval, daughters of the murdered Prime Minister.

It was this sunny nature that caused him to be a favourite almost wherever he went, and that opened to him the doors of so many aristocratic houses. It was next to impossible for dulness to reign where he was. "Gloom could not long prevail in presence of his invariable cheerfulness," notes one of his sons. He adds: "I never knew anyone else so quick of perception, and so intensely rapid in thought and action, and at the same time so uniformly bright and happy."

In regard to his facial characteristics, I have the further note: "His features were very pronounced, and he possessed a sharp dark brown eye."

With such a nature and disposition one can well believe that the artist was one of the "live" members of the "Widows' Club," composed of some of the leading wits and "characters" of the day, which had its home in a public-house opposite to Aldridges', in St. Martin's Lane. Amongst other members were Edmund Kean, William Linton, "Jerry Sneak" Russell, the actor (so called from a part he played to perfection); David Roberts, R.A., Clarkson

Stanfield, R.A., Nugent, a writer for the *Times;* and Turner, the animal painter.

The latter had a wooden leg and was one of the butts of the club. Once, when Linton was in the chair, Turner was very persistent in calling his attention to some remark he wished to make, and kept rising and shouting, "Mr. Linton! Mr. Linton!" At length Linton knocked loudly on the table, and called his fellow-guests' attention by saying, "Gentlemen, attention, please, for Mr. Turner, who is on his leg." Turner's eagerness subsided at once, and he sank into his chair and was silent for the rest of the evening.

On another occasion, when the confraternity were about to disperse, and Turner was found to be fast asleep in his chair, they wheeled him in front of the fire, stuck the end of his wooden leg between the bars, and there left him. When he awoke several inches of his timber "understanding" had been burned off. He used to say that he was awakened by feeling his toes burning.

This sort of practical joking was very prevalent at the time, and formed one of the most common amusements of both high and low. Kean, however, served the wooden-legged painter a trick that was hardly fair. Turner left the club along with the tragedian, and was persistent in his efforts to hang on to him, hobbling along behind and calling out, "Mr. Kean! Mr. Kean! I say, Mr. Kean!" Kean had no desire for his company, and did not wish to be followed. Finding, therefore, that he could not get rid of the painter, he stopped a policeman, gave him his name, and bade him look after poor Turner, saying, "He has been following me for this ten minutes, and I fear can't be up to any good."

When in 1821 the Society of Painters in Oil and Water Colours was going back to its old limits of a society for water colourists only, Holmes was beginning to abandon that branch of art in favour of oils—a medium in which he never appeared to so good an advantage as in water colours. For this reason it was that he did not exhibit any picture in 1821.

He subsequently exerted the whole of his influence towards the founding of the Society of British Artists, which held its first exhibition in 1824. He was a constant exhibitor with that society for a period of nearly thirty years, both in "subject" and portraiture.

Heaphy was the first president of the society. Holmes followed him in that office soon after (1829).

George Robson, the water-colour painter and a member of the Water Colour Society, thought

Holmes did wrong to leave that society, and used to tell him he was never satisfied; he was always hankering after something new. In this respect he differed very much from Robson, who was, perhaps, as steady-going as Holmes was erratic. The latter was for many years on terms of great intimacy with Robson, whose work he greatly admired. Robson was a man of great energy and much originality. It is said of him that he was so determined as a boy to devote himself to art that nothing could repress him; and at sixteen years of age he set out from his home (in Durham) for London with five pounds in his pocket. But so well did he make his way that, during his first year in the metropolis, he was able to return the five pounds to his father. This was about the year 1807; in 1814 he was elected a member of the Water Colour Society, of which he became president in 1820. A curious story is told in regard to his death, which occurred in 1833. While going by steamboat to visit his friends in the North, he was taken seriously ill and had to be landed at Stockton-on-Tees. Others fell sick at the same time, though not so seriously as he; the result, it is said, of eating food that had been cooked in a copper utensil that had not been properly cleaned. He never recovered, and his last words were, " I am poisoned." The curious part of the story, however, is that some years after his reported death the sons of his old friend Holmes went to stay at a place in Devonshire where Robson had been in the habit of putting up ; and in the course of conversation one of them said to the landlady, " You have, of course, heard of the sad death of poor Mr. Robson by poison on board ship as he was on his way North ?" " Oh dear, no, that's all a mistake," replied the old lady. " Mr. Robson was here only a few months ago, and stayed several weeks with us. He was never better in his life, or looked less like dying." And nothing could persuade the good creature that such was not the case.

It was about this time (1823 or 1824) that Holmes became acquainted with a man of his own profession with whom he remained in the closest ties of friend-ship till death came to separate them. This was Frederick Yeates Hurlstone, a painter now almost forgotten, but in his day looked up to by many of his brother artists as of the first rank. Indeed, but the other day one who remembered him well re-marked that " he was the only British artist who held his own at the International Exhibition of 1862."

Hurlstone's father was a writer, and was on the

staff of the *Morning Herald*, in connection with which he used to tell an amusing story. The *Herald* was supported by members of the Government, and one large contributor to the funds had his nephew, a young sprig of aristocracy, placed on the staff of the paper. But he proved to be a terrible plague; everything he wrote caused trouble, whether it was on politics, social matters, religion, or what not; and at last, at a meeting of the Board, it was bluntly said that he must be got rid of, or the paper would be ruined. "You can't get rid of him," said the chairman; "his uncle is in the Government." "What can we do then?" asked the others. No one could tell. At length one of the directors, who had hitherto remained silent, smilingly said, "I will tell you how to get out of the difficulty." "How?" asked the others eagerly. "Make him the art critic," was the reply. "But he knows nothing about art," they all said. "So much the better," returned the one who had proposed that way out of the difficulty. Finally, after some talk, this advice was taken, the paper was saved, and the young gentleman got a post in which he worked to his own entire satisfaction, and to the no small content of those who worked with him.

Hurlstone was introduced to Holmes by Mr. Rudall, the flautist. He had a little while before

(1823) taken the Royal Academy gold medal for historical painting, the subject being "The Contention between the Archangel Michael and Satan for the Body of Moses." There was some disinclination to award him the medal because the picture was not considered academical enough in style, but its undoubted great qualities, including fine colour, carried the day. It is not very creditable to the artist's sons to learn that this noted picture was allowed to rot away in a damp cellar.

When Holmes and Hurlstone first became acquainted the latter had just commenced portrait painting, and was living in Howland Street, Fitzroy Square, being consequently a near neighbour of Holmes. He subsequently acquired an extensive practice as a portrait-painter. He used to take his first rough sketch of a sitter in Indian red, black and white, and in the course of an hour or two would get a very effective outline, using the red pure here and there, and especially to mark in the line of the jaw, the nose, etc. He used this method in painting the portrait of Malibran, who, upon seeing the red and black strongly laid in, observed, "Ah, Mr. Hailstone, I see you put in the bones and muscles first, and of course you will place the skin on afterwards."

In 1835 Hurlstone went to Italy, Holmes

accompanying him as far as Milan. He remained for some time in Rome, where he at once began to study and produce pictures of boy-life in the Eternal City that soon placed him in the front rank of his profession.

He subsequently visited Spain and Morocco. While in the latter country he painted his "Last Sigh of Boabdil," or a large portion of it. He experienced a difficulty in getting models; but finally one morning, as he was painting in his studio, he was startled by hearing the voice of his dragoman from the courtyard crying out, "Master, come! Master, come and help me! Master, quick, quick!" Running down in great haste to see what was the matter, Hurlstone saw his man struggling with a couple of natives, whom he had dragged into the court and was trying to get into the house. Being aware of his master's dilemma, and not knowing how to procure models in any other way, he had laid hold of these men in the street and was bringing them in against their will. But they kicked up such a hullabaloo that Hurlstone had to give them money to pacify them, fearing a disturbance by the people. By this means, however, they were finally won, and the painter got all the sittings he wanted.

Hurlstone's weak point as an artist was in

regard to composition, in which he used to seek Holmes's advice. But he was a splendid colourist; he drew the head well; and there was a fine daring about his work. These qualities were recognised by Mr. Whistler when, happening to drop one day into Mr. George Holmes's studio, he saw Hurlstone's "Gil Blas and the Canon Sedillo" standing against an easel.

"Ah!" exclaimed the worthy M'Neil, raising his glass to his eye *more suo*, "Ah, an excellent bit of work that—very excellent! Who is the painter?"

"Hurlstone," replied Mr. Holmes. "It did not sell, and so I purchased it of the artist's sons."

"Sell! sell!" lisped Mr. Whistler. "Of course it did not sell: it is much too good."

There are many amusing stories told of Hurlstone, who was quite a character in his way. He painted with so much haste and vigour, blowing and hissing through his teeth the while, that artists used to say, "He works away as though he were grooming a horse." On one occasion a big blue-bottle fly flew against his canvas and stuck to the wet paint, but so great was the fury of the artist's industry that he could not spare time to take it off, and so worked it up with his brush and allowed it to go as a bit of body-colour. Someone asked him why he did not take it off. "No time—it all helps!" was the reply.

Like Turner, he was always abused by the critics, who seldom understand original men.

In his later years Hurlstone showed signs of becoming insane in regard to money. He was always rather avaricious and miserly, and when his sons were growing up he often complained to Holmes that they would not work.

"Work! of course not," replied his friend. "They know you are rich, and that they won't need to do so."

"But I'm not rich," said Hurlstone.

"They know better; make up your mind to that. If they did not, they would work. My sons have no doubt as to my poverty, and they work."

As a matter of fact, Hurlstone left his sons very well off, but his hardly-accumulated wealth seemed to do them very little good, and one, if not both, died in the greatest poverty. One, indeed, was reduced to the extremity of becoming a kerbstone musician.

Among leading contemporary artists there were few that were not known to Holmes. He was well acquainted with David Cox, both of them being members of the Water Colour Society; and on one occasion Cox made him a sketch of a cottage for his picture of "Boys going to School."

He used to meet Turner on the committee of the Artists' General Benevolent Fund, of which Holmes was a member, and they were on very friendly terms. On one occasion the case came up of an old lady who applied for relief. Turner asked what she had done. Someone said she had once painted some flowers. "That won't do," replied Turner; "to have once painted some flowers is not enough to entitle her to relief."

"Oh, give her a couple of guineas for some snuff and tuppany," suggested Holmes. "Very well," acquiesced Turner, "give her a couple of guineas; but I tell you what it is, Mr. Holmes, if you had the management of this fund there would soon be an end of it."

This was characteristic of Holmes. Although in the receipt of a good income, amounting at the best times to 2000 guineas or more per annum, yet he was always in need of money. He once told Linnell that an artist could not save on £2000 a year;[1] and certainly he did not arrive at the achievement himself.

Once he asked Sir Henry Meux, for whom he was at the time executing many commissions, for

[1] Linnell told him he would put by 1s. out of £20 a year.

an advance.   Said Sir Henry in reply, "It is no business of mine, Mr. Holmes, but how do you manage to get through your money?   It is only a short time since you had a large sum from me." "I really don't know, I'm sure," replied Holmes. "It goes somehow.   There always seem to be no end of expenses."

It is the more difficult to understand what he did with his money, because at a time when hard drinking was the custom, he was always a temperate man ; nor was he addicted to any special extravagance in other directions.   But the fact is—and this is the only explanation in such cases as his— that he had "a hole in his pocket," and when he received a cheque the money soon found its way through the aperture.

Hawkins, a sort of assistant and hanger-on, used to say that no sooner had Holmes received a cheque than he would say, "I've received a cheque, Hawkins ; come along and I'll change it.   Is there anything I want ? "

"No, I don't think there is," Hawkins would reply ; "you seem to have everything you need."

"Never mind ! Come along, it must be changed," was the artist's almost invariable response.

Of Turner Holmes used to declare that he saw nothing in his face indicative of genius or of great.

intelligence except his bright, piercing eye. "He had," he was wont to say, "a glance of almost preternatural keenness."

Everyone noticed that exceptional quality. William Westall was accustomed to relate how Turner's look went through him when, on one occasion, seeing a picture of the master's in which he had painted a palm-tree yellow, he ventured to approach the famous painter with trepidation and apologies, and inform him that a palm-tree was never yellow. "I have travelled a great deal in the East, Mr. Turner," he went on, "and therefore I know of what I am speaking; and I can assure you that a palm-tree is never of that colour; it is always green." "Umph!" grunted Turner, almost transfixing him with his glance. "Umph! I can't afford it—can't afford it;" and with these words he walked away. "I felt under his steady gaze," said Westall, when relating the incident,—"I felt that it was quite immaterial what colour it was in nature, so long as he desired it different, and I think I could have sworn that it was different when under his eye."

Another anecdote of Turner may fittingly come in here. On one occasion Lee exhibited a farm-house on fire. On varnishing day the Academicians gathered round it, as is their custom, and passed their criticisms. Landseer, amongst others, made his suggestions, and also put a dab of his brush in it. Then Turner approached, and Lee said, "Ah, here is Mr. Turner, but he never has anything to say." "Put more fire in your house," said the master, and passed on. It was not half blazing enough for him.

CHAPTER XII

MENTION has already been made of Sir Henry
Meux (of the firm of brewers of that name) as
being amongst the number of Holmes's patrons
during the later years of George IV and the
earlier part of the reign of William.   Sir Henry
was a great admirer of his friend's talents, and his
mansion at Theobalds, near Edgeware, was largely
decorated by his pencil.   For a long time the artist
enjoyed a commission for one picture a year, besides
portraits.

He was a frequent and honoured guest at
Theobalds, where he met many celebrated men,
including some of the leading wits and politicians
of the time.   Amongst others he frequently had
the pleasure of meeting Lord Brougham, whose
description of breakfast as a "skirmishing meal"
greatly amused him.

There it was that he first met Abraham Cooper,

R.A.   Abraham had formerly been a groom in Sir Henry's stables, and owed his rise very much to his master's kindness and patronage.   Seeing once the drawing of a horse on his stable door, Sir Henry remarked to his stableman, " Surely that must be meant for So-and-so," mentioning the name of one of his horses.

" It is," said the stableman.

" Who did it ? "

The stableman replied that it was the work of the lad Cooper. Questioned further, he said that the youth was always drawing, and seemed very clever at it.

Sir Henry sent for Cooper, questioned him, and finished by asking him if he would like to learn to paint.   Cooper replied that he would, whereupon Sir Henry gave him money to buy brushes, paints, etc. ; in short, started him upon his career.

As it was the drawing of a horse that first called attention to his budding gifts, so it was the portrait of a horse that first brought him into public notice. This was in 1809, when he was about twenty-five years of age.   Some years later he won the premium of the British Institution for his finished sketch of the " Battle of Ligny."

It was during this period of Holmes's intimacy

with Meux that a large ale-vat in the firm's brewery at the corner of Tottenham Court Road burst, and, as is said, flooded the adjacent streets. At that time New Oxford Street had not been formed, and the labyrinth of courts and lanes through which it was afterwards cut was known as Little Hell. It was into this minor Inferno that the flood descended, and Holmes often told how he saw the squalid denizens prone upon their bellies drinking the ale from the gutters till they were dead drunk.

The artist used to relate an incident in the life of Sir Henry Meux that is rather striking. Early in his career he was involved in a lawsuit, the loss of which would have carried with it the loss of the brewery, and indeed reduced him to poverty. Fortunately, judgment was given in his favour. So doubtful, however, was the issue (and when is not law doubtful?), and so great Sir Henry's anxiety, that, on the last day of the trial, he went into court with a loaded pistol in his pocket, determined, if he lost the case, to put an end to his life.

Many of the artist's pictures, as well of course as his portraits, still adorn the walls of Theobalds, as well as the town house of the Meuxes.

Another rich art patron with whom Holmes was intimate at this time, although I am not sure that he had any commission from him, was Mr. Hope, the well-known virtuoso, who inherited from his father, John Williams Hope, head of the famous banking house of Amsterdam, an immense fortune and estates in Cornwall. He spent large sums of money on pictures, besides indulging an extravagant taste for diamonds, which he was not ashamed of wearing plentifully upon his person. He showed a somewhat effeminate taste in other matters also; and amongst his many oddities possessed that of being generally averse to male society. In Paris, where he spent the latter part of his life, he formed a coterie of eighteen ladies distinguished for their artistic or musical gifts. When one died or quitted the society she was replaced by another, but the number eighteen was never exceeded. He was noted for his princely hospitality as well as for his eccentricity, and his mansion in the Faubourg St. Germain was among the best known in fashionable circles in Paris. His collection of pictures was one of the largest in the world owned by a private person. These and his other works of art were on his death dispersed by auction.

When in London Holmes frequently met Mr. Hope at his house in Harley Street, where it was the rule to meet the nicest people and eat the choicest of dinners.

On one occasion when there the artist noticed a portrait by Joseph of Mr. Spencer Perceval, the Prime Minister who was assassinated (in 1812) as he was coming out of the House of Commons by the man Bellingham.

"I see you have got a portrait of Mr. Perceval by my friend Joseph," Holmes observed.

"Yes," returned Mr. Hope. "You know him then?"

Holmes replied that he did, adding that he liked Joseph very much, that he was a very agreeable man, and so forth.

"Oh yes," responded Mr. Hope. "Joseph is a very nice man—a very nice man indeed; but there is one thing about him that you may possibly not have remarked."

"What is that?" asked Holmes.

"That, Academician though he be, he can't paint."

"Oh, that's nothing," replied Holmes. "It's a failing with a lot of them."

Mr. Hope's portrait of Mr. Perceval was doubtless one of a large order which Joseph received. He used to boast that he had been the recipient of the largest portrait commission that was ever given to one man: this was to paint fifty portraits of the murdered Premier.

So great was the indignation caused throughout the country by the crime that a subscription was started, and associations formed, to perpetuate Mr. Perceval's memory; and Joseph's portrait commission was one of the forms the memorial took, each person or association subscribing so much being entitled to a copy of the likeness. Nor was the price, fifty guineas per portrait, bad for those days.

Prices were then very different from what they are now, both for portraits and for pictures. Holmes painted a replica of his " Boy going to School" for Mr. Chamberlayne, for which he asked £120. Chamberlayne demurred at first, saying he never gave more than £100 for a water-colour drawing, but finally paid the price asked.

Once when Holmes and Richter were walking out together, they met Joseph, who had just been elected an Academician. They congratulated him, saying they had but now heard of the honour conferred upon him. "Yes," he said, "it is true I have been elected an Academician, and that notwithstanding I won the gold medal."

It was a tradition in those days that a man who won the Academy's gold medal never became an Academician. Joseph gained the gold medal in 1792 for a " Scene from Coriolanus." His election as an associate took place in 1813.

There were very few notable or notorious persons of that day, male or female, that the artist was not brought in contact with, either professionally or otherwise, and he was as ready to smile at their foibles as to condole with them in their distresses.

"He is proud of his wound," he remarked of Lord Castlereagh, when that nobleman called upon him with his arm in a sling after his duel with Signor Melcy, the husband of Grisi. The quarrel arose out of the nobleman's attentions to the songstress. Melcy was very vicious and aimed at his opponent's heart, intending to kill him. Castlereagh, on the contrary, had no desire to hurt his antagonist, and pointed his pistol in the air. The act probably saved his life, Melcy's bullet striking his elbow and running up his arm to the shoulder.

It was remarked at the time that Castlereagh's arm was an unconscionably long time getting well, and that he paraded a good deal up and down the Mall with the injured member in a sling. He sat to Holmes for his portrait during its mending.

Another society scandal of the time exercised the artist's feelings in a different way. This was the elopement of the beautiful Lady Ellenborough, wife of Lord Ellenborough, sometime Governor-General of India, with Prince Schwarzenberg, an *attaché* of the Austrian embassy in London, and subsequently

Austrian Prime Minister. Holmes knew the lady, as well as her father, Admiral Digby, well, and had painted two portraits of her, one as a child and another just before the elopement. Prince Schwarzenberg was making frequent calls on the artist during the sittings for the latter, and it would appear that while his visits were ostensibly intended for Holmes, they were virtually made in order to get speech with the lady.

Society was greatly scandalized by the event, and the marriage was annulled by a special Act of Parliament. This was in 1830.

Twenty years afterwards the divorced wife called upon Mr. Holmes to introduce to him her new husband, Count Theoroky, a Greek nobleman. She then told her old friend how scandalously Schwarzenberg had treated her, deserting her in Paris, whither they had gone on quitting England, without a shilling. The recollection of his heart-lessness was still so poignant that she wept over the recital.

At this time Holmes painted a third portrait of her.

A celebrity of a very different character with whom the artist had become acquainted a little before this time was the Earl of Dundonald, whose career is one of the most romantic in the long and brilliant roll of our naval heroes. He possessed unfortunately, in conjunction with a coolness and daring that was never excelled, an impatience and intolerance of wrongdoing that brought him into constant conflict with his superiors and the corrupt governments of those days. Both in the House of Commons, to which he was elected as a member for Westminster along with Sir Francis Burdett, and by pamphlet he exposed and attacked the abuses of the naval administration, and by that means made himself obnoxious to the Admiralty and the authorities generally.

He gave further offence by charging Lord Gambier, his superior officer, with neglect of duty (which was true), and by denouncing the abuses of the prize-court and the treatment of prisoners of war.

Unfortunately an opportunity soon (1814) occurred for his enemies to wreak their revenge upon him. They succeeded in convicting him on a charge—afterwards proved to be false—of originating a rumour for speculative purposes that Napoleon had abdicated. He was expelled from Parliament, deprived of all his honours, sent to prison for a year, and condemned to pay a fine of £1000. As a further punishment he was required to stand in the pillory, exposed to the gibes of the populace. This last indignity, however, was spared him; his colleague in the representation of Westminster, Sir Francis Burdett, saying that he would stand with him if that part of the sentence were enforced.

The electors of Westminster immediately subscribed the money to pay his fine and re-elected him, but he had to remain in prison till the expiration of his sentence.

In June 1815 Lord Cochrane (as he then was) was told that, his term of imprisonment having expired, he would be set at liberty on payment of the fine of £1000. At first he refused to be set free on this condition, but finally, on the 13th of July, he accepted his liberty, paying the fine with a banknote on the back of which he wrote: " My health having suffered during my long and close confinement, and my pursuers having resolved to deprive me of property or life, I submit to robbery to protect myself from murder, in the hope that I shall live to bring the delinquents to justice." This note is still preserved amongst the archives of the Bank of England.

He was subsequently tried and again imprisoned because he would not pay a fine of £100. The people were so strongly roused by the injustice and persecution to which he was subjected that the £100 was raised by a penny subscription. Then, so popular was the movement, that the subscription was continued and the original fine of £1000, together with the costs of his defence, was paid by it.

In 1817, in response to the invitation of the leaders of the newly-established Republic of Chili, Dundonald accepted the command of its navy, and did so well for them that to him is due perhaps more than to any other man the ultimate independence of that country. He subsequently did the same service for Brazil.

In 1832 he was restored to his rank in the British navy, and died Rear-Admiral of the United Kingdom. Dundonald did much to promote the adoption of steam and the screw-propeller in war ships.

A close friendship subsisted between him and the artist for a long series of years, ending only with the death of the former in 1860. Holmes painted two portraits of his friend, one of them as late as 1846, which should still be among the heirlooms of the Cochrane family.

CHAPTER XIII

A FAMOUS SMUGGLER

HOLMES seems to have had the faculty of attracting about him the strangest oddities and eccentricities of character. Amongst the number of these was Captain Johnson, a famous smuggler of the early part of the century, when, in consequence of the general upset and confusion arising from the protracted wars, smuggling between France and England, and indeed all along the French and Dutch coasts, was carried on to an enormous extent.

Captain Johnson was one of the most noted and notorious of the men occupied in this nefarious business. He had a vessel of his own, was a man of iron nerve, and of great intrepidity of character, full of resource and daring to the last degree. His long experience in the trade had made him intimately and minutely acquainted with the French and Dutch coasts. Indeed, so well was he versed in the intricacies of the latter, that he was employed as pilot in the ill-fated Walcheren expedition; an officer standing over him with a loaded pistol as he gave his directions, ready to blow his brains out if he showed the least indication of treachery.

Thrice Johnson broke out of London prisons, his most daring escape being from Horsemonger Jail. It shows the lawlessness of the times that he could manage to do so with such comparative ease. Friends outside were in the secret of the intended attempt, and a postchaise was in readiness near the prison, to convey him to Dover.

The attempt took place early in the morning. The prisoner had been clandestinely supplied with pistols. His cell was shared by a companion. Johnson said to him, "Do you feel inclined to go out to-day? I intend to do so."

The man said he should like to get away.

"Then," said Johnson, "follow my example," at the same time giving him a pistol.

When the turnkey entered, Johnson drew his pistol, and presenting it at his head, bade him open the door if he did not want to be a dead man. The fellow obeyed, and the two prisoners were soon outside the walls and driving post-haste to Dover.

Mr. Thomas Frost, in his *Reminiscences of a Country Journalist*, gives the following additional details of this prison-breaking exploit: " All arrangements for Johnson's escape from prison and his flight to the Continent had been made beforehand, and a large number of persons must have been in the secret, yet the whole plan was successfully carried out without a hitch. A postchaise awaited him near the prison, relays of horses being in readiness at every stage between London and Dover; the turnpike gates were thrown open at his approach, and a fast-sailing lugger was lying off the coast with her sails set and anchor weighed by the time he reached it. 'Guineas flew right and left,' as my father expressed it, to secure the smuggler's escape."

Such an exploit in broad daylight in London seems hardly possible—at least to us of to-day. But, in order to make it conceivable, we have only to bear in mind the changed aspect of things since the beginning of the century. The entire condition and aspect of society have changed so materially that we might almost be in another world.

On another occasion Johnson broke out of Fleet Prison, tearing up his bedclothes to make ropes, and descending hand over hand from the roof to the street.

When advancing age made it incumbent upon him to settle down as a simple citizen, Johnson used often to speak of the adventures and hairbreadth escapes of his earlier manhood, when half the time he seemed to carry his life in his hand.

Asked once whither he went after breaking out of Fleet Prison, he said he went and took breakfast with his wife in Bloomsbury Square. He knew, he said, that they would never seek him in his own house.

At this time Johnson was comparatively a rich man, the profits on a successful smuggling operation being enormous.

On one occasion he is said to have cleared as much as £20,000 from one trip across the Channel. The trade was the more profitable because the French connived at it. It was for this reason probably that Johnson was as well known to the French authorities as he was to the English.

With the former his reputation for daring and intrepidity, as well as for seamanship, was so great that he was once offered the command of a French man-of-war. He was lying in a Dutch prison for some smuggling escapade when the offer was made. An officer entered, and looking round and seeing no one but a man on his knees washing the floor of the cell, he asked where he could see Captain Johnson.

"I am Captain Johnson," said the man, intermitting his work and looking up.

The officer, after taking a good look at him,

asked him whether, on condition of being set at liberty, he would take command of a French vessel.

Johnson reflected for a minute or two. He knew that it meant fighting against his own people, and in open war. He did not quite fall in with the idea, and therefore replied that he should like to have a few days to consider the matter. This delay was accorded; and Johnson at once wrote a letter to Lord Sidmouth,[1] telling him of the offer that had been made to him, and explaining that, while he would rather not fight against his native country, yet he had his wife and children to think of, and was therefore prepared to refuse to accept the command on condition of being given a free pardon for his offences against the laws of his country in regard to smuggling.

The letter was despatched to London by means of some of his trusty smuggling friends, and in due course, by the same channel, an answer was returned, granting him the pardon he asked.

Upon the receipt of this document Johnson resolved to escape from his prison and get back to England as soon as possible. He quickly found a way to do so, hiding securely, when he had succeeded, in

---

[1] Lord Sidmouth became Lord President of the Council in 1805 under Pitt, and in 1812, under Lord Liverpool's administration, he was Secretary of State for the Home Department.

a house next door to the jail, until such time as an opportunity afforded of getting a passage home.

He appears subsequently to have been in the pay of the Government, as a secret-service agent or something of the kind, as he used often, when he called at Holmes's studio, to say that he was going to the Horse Guards to see the Duke of York, sometimes showing papers which he intimated were of importance to the Commander-in-Chief. Unless he had been useful to the Government in some such way, it is hardly likely that, notorious smuggler as he had been, he would have died in the enjoyment of a Government pension. Nominally, however, I believe it was given to him for having conducted the Walcheren expedition, although the service then rendered was hardly sufficient to warrant such a reward.

One of Johnson's last schemes was to build a submarine boat with which to rescue Napoleon from his imprisonment on the Island of St. Helena. His idea was to construct such a craft as could be propelled for a certain distance under water, and by that means elude the vigilance of the men-of-war guarding the island; then having reached the shore, take off the prisoner, and by descending again under water, reach a vessel far out at sea, in waiting to proceed with the rescued Emperor to Europe.

According to his own statement, Johnson must have been in connivance with influential friends of Napoleon to effect this purpose, as he used to tell Holmes, and Hawkins, the artist above referred to, who was wont to act as his assistant, that if he effected his purpose it would be worth half a million of money to him.

However, the scheme proved abortive. The boat, which was being constructed on the Thames, was one day quietly seized by custom-house officers, and no more was heard of it.

Johnson and Hawkins, through meeting at Holmes's house, became very close friends; and up to the day of his death, not many years ago, Hawkins was never tired of talking about Johnson and the various adventures and escapades that he had from time to time described to him.

On one occasion the latter was lodged in the King's Bench Prison for debt. Hawkins asked him why he did not escape, as he had done so often enough before. " Ah," Johnson replied, "times are changed. Besides, I am not so young as I was."

Hawkins, as a young man, gave great promise of future eminence—a promise which was not fulfilled however. "Could Hawkins ever paint?" Holmes was once asked. "Oh yes," he replied, "when he was twenty. Once he painted very well indeed, and we thought he was going to do something great—become a Michael Angelo, or something of the kind. But he has been steadily going back ever since."

Perhaps the mischief lay in the fact that he was so good a companion as to be much sought after by men who wanted to be amused, and the artist was only too ready to fall into their humour. On one occasion he was asked by a Mr. Ackers, a member of Parliament, now pretty well forgotten, like so many others, to accompany him and one or two others to Paris, promising to give him a holiday and pay all his expenses. Hawkins objected, saying that he was busy on a picture which he wanted to finish for exhibition. "Never mind that," said Ackers. "Bring it with you and paint there." Hawkins yielded and the canvas was put into the carriage. As they were driving along, Mr. Ackers asked to be allowed to look at the picture. It was accordingly uncovered. "What do you want for it?" he asked. "I shall want £50 for it when it is finished," said Hawkins. "Very well," replied the member of Parliament, "I will give it you, and will finish it for you too." With these words he kicked a hole right through the canvas.

Hawkins died in a poor lodging in Camden Town, at an advanced age. He had never known

what it was to be in easy or even in fairly comfortable circumstances; but he was of an easy-going,
good-natured disposition, and had been lucky enough
to have had many good friends, who sought him out
for his amiable and amusing ways. When he was
on his death-bed, one of the sons of his former
master said, " Well, Hawkins, you have had a long
life ; how have you enjoyed it ?" " Oh," he replied,
"it has been a charming existence. I have done
such splendid work, have had so much praise, and
have lived in the best society, that it has been
perfectly delightful."

"A good instance," observed the narrator, "of
how a man may live and be happy in a fool's
paradise."

The fact is that Hawkins, whatever he may have
been able to do at the age of twenty-one, was never
after able to paint the least bit. He could not be
brought to recognise his incapacity, however, and
continued to the end to believe in his own great
achievements.

One story that he was never tired of telling was
how he was one day met by William Linton, the
sculptor, who asked him where he had been, as he
had not seen him for some time. Hawkins replied
that he had been in Hertfordshire (which was his
native county, and where he had friends), and that

he had been painting portraits; adding that in Hertfordshire they thought a great deal of his portraits. "Ah, yes, of course," replied Linton, "and very properly too, for everybody knows you are the Hertfordshire Vandyke." The name of the Hertfordshire Vandyke stuck to Hawkins ever afterwards; and he himself was not the least ready to style himself by that title.

Holmes used to say that it was impossible to kill Hawkins; he was bound to achieve old age and die in his bed, which, in fact, he did, passing away at over eighty years of age. He had many narrow escapes of his life, but always came out safe and sound. One day a big door fell upon him, that would certainly have killed another and lesser man; another time he was overturned in a coach. Once he went out swimming at Weymouth, and never thought of the turning tide till he found himself far away from shore, with the sea running swiftly out. He owed his life to being perceived by some coast-guardsmen. When he was telling some of his friends of the narrow escape of drowning he had had, they replied, "Oh no, we know better than that. A man who is born to be hanged cannot be drowned." And so, nearly always the butt of jest and merriment, Hawkins was always happy.

One of the artist's sons, Mr. Edward Holmes,

used to tell an amusing anecdote of a daughter of his father's old friend Johnson. He met her one day, long after her father's death, in Hyde Park. She was then trying to earn a living by teaching the guitar, and explained that she had put an advertisement in the *Morning Post* to the effect that a daughter of the late Captain Johnson, the famous smuggler, wished to find pupils for instruction on the guitar, and hoped that it might be the means of bringing her business. Mr. Holmes rather discouraged her by saying that he feared it might have the opposite effect to the one she hoped, at the same time reminding her how much the times had changed since her father was regarded as a sort of popular hero.

CHAPTER XIV

AN UNLUCKY AND A LUCKY ARTIST

In 1835 occurred the brief visit to Italy, along with Hurlstone, already referred to. It lasted barely two months, and does not appear to have had any effect in stimulating new work. The friends journeyed together as far as Milan, whence Holmes proceeded to Venice, attracted thither probably by a desire to witness the scenes amidst which his friend Byron had passed so many of his later years. After spending some time there and making a few studies, he went back to Milan, where he made a short stay, and then returned home.

He continued to exhibit with the British Artists until 1850, when he resigned his membership of the Society.

In 1843 he paid a visit, extending over a few months, to Ireland. He was the guest of Mr. Maxwell, of Co. Louth. While there he was for a short time also the guest of the Earl of Kingston,

who was an old friend. At his table he once met
Father Mathew, the great Apostle of Temperance,
in whom he became much interested. Seated next
to him at dinner, he said, " Mr. Mathew, I should
be pleased to drink wine with you." " I shall be
most happy," said Father Mathew. With that he
poured out a glass of water, saying with a smile,
" This is my vintage—a very old and safe one.
Your very good health, Mr. Holmes ! "

" A splendid man ! " was the artist's comment.
" A fine handsome face, healthy, good colour,
beaming with good-nature ; but how he could keep
it up on water God only knows ! "

During his stay at Lord Kingston's he paid a
hasty visit to the Lakes of Killarney, and made a
number of sketches ; but he does not appear to
have done anything further with them.

In 1846 died Haydon by his own hand. Holmes
was greatly shocked to learn the sad tidings. He
had known Haydon from his very early days, and
had a great appreciation of his talents, considering
him one of the greatest historical painters of the
time. But so lacking in tact was poor Haydon, and
so wanting in all those qualities of the heart that
constitute half the battle in enabling men to win
their way, that he failed practically in everything he
undertook, and in nothing so signally as in his

attempt to start a school in opposition to the Royal Academy.

In his hostility to the Academy he had Holmes's entire sympathy, as well as that of Hurlstone.

Both Holmes and Hurlstone were always hostile to that institution, and rarely sent either pictures or portraits to it. Holmes stigmatized it as a "close borough," and used to express his wonder to Linnell that he should contribute to its exhibitions. Linnell's answer was that, though the Academy had its faults, so had the other societies, and in larger measure. Hurlstone was for ever warring against it.

One of the most astonishing things about Haydon's career is that he won the affection of so few and the hatred of so many. In some cases the latter feeling can only have betokened a narrow and unsympathetic nature. John Linnell, for instance, used to relate how he once met Sass, who kept a drawing school in St. Martin's Lane—and a famous one in its time—as he was going into Covent Garden Theatre, and Sass immediately began to relate how Haydon had that afternoon called upon him and asked for a trifling loan.

"And what did you say?" asked Linnell.

"I said," replied the little drawing master, "that if the schoolroom was filled so full from floor to ceiling with golden sovereigns that not another could be got in, I would not lend him a single one, no, nor half of one, if it were to save his life.   And I wouldn't, the wretch!"

As he was uttering the last words Haydon stalked past them into the theatre, not deigning to notice the spiteful little viper.

Holmes used to tell the following story of poor Haydon.   Calling one day on "Roman" Davies (so called in contradistinction to Richard Davies, the animal painter, and brother of the well-known Queen's huntsman) to see his just completed picture of "The Lord Mayor visiting the Sick at the Time of the Plague," Holmes found that artist sorely perplexed over a note which he had just received by the twopenny post from Haydon.   Davies had earlier in the day received a visit from that gentleman, who expressed himself as being much pleased with the work, although he made some slight criticisms upon the Lord Mayor's horse.   One may imagine his surprise therefore when he read the following brief epistle :—

My dear Davies—Go instantly and dissect a horse.—Yours faithfully,   W. B. Haydon.

Handing the precious document to Holmes, Davies questioned hopelessly—

"How can I do as he says?   The picture goes away to-morrow."

"Oh, it's only one of Haydon's after-thoughts," laughed Holmes. "Take no notice of it—till you get a commission for a replica."

It was during these years, that is, early in the forties, that Holmes was invited by the Duke of Wellington to call upon him with a view to painting a portrait of him. He met the Duke at the Countess of Jersey's. His Grace was then about to go over to Paris on some diplomatic business, but said he should be pleased to see him at Apsley House when he returned. The artist happened to be away when he did return, and so the opportunity passed, or he failed to seize it, much to his subsequent regret.

Lady Jersey was a good patron of his and brought him many commissions. She also sat for her own portrait, and took her coronet to Wilton Street in order to be painted in it. The coronet remained there for some time afterwards as a memento of the person and the occasion; and the two surviving sons of the artist have still a vivid recollection of its crimson velvet magnificence.

Another artist contemporary with whom Holmes was well acquainted, and of whom an infinite number of jests used to be related, was William Tassie, the modeller and reproducer of antique gems. He was not so great an artist as his uncle, Robert Tassie, whose pupil he was, and to whom he succeeded in the business the former had established in Leicester Square (on the site now occupied by the Hotel Cavour), but he was a notable man in his day, and as pious as he was clever. Of his cleverness, or rather, one should say, of his resourcefulness, an interesting instance is recorded. He had received a command to attend on George IV and model his portrait. While waiting in an anteroom of the palace he discovered that in the flurry of the moment he had forgotten to bring with him one of his favourite smaller modelling tools that was essential to the work in hand. There being no time to go back for it, the artist was at first in despair; then, with ready inventiveness, he took out a pocket-comb he was in the habit of carrying, broke off one of its teeth, and with this improvised instrument modelled the medallion.

Tassie was of a generous and considerate turn, and once at least his good-nature met with a curious and most unexpected reward. An impecunious artist had one day come to him bemoaning his imprudence in having invested a much-needed guinea in a ticket for the lottery by means of which Boydell's Shakespeare Gallery was to be disposed of. Tassie, in pity for his distress, bought the ticket from him, but not without giving him a grave lecture on the folly of such extravagance. The lottery was drawn for on the 28th of January 1805, and out of 22,000 tickets sold, that held by William Tassie won the chief prize, which included the Shakespeare Gallery, pictures, and estate! After making a present to the artist who had been the original owner of the ticket, Tassie sold his winnings by auction, the works of art realising over £6180, the Gallery itself being purchased by the British Institution.

The day after Tassie drew this lucky prize, of which everybody naturally was talking, Holmes met him, and at once congratulated him on his good fortune.

"An astounding piece of luck, Mr. Tassie!" he exclaimed, in his impulsive, jocular way. "All we other poor devils of artists are quite envying you. We would like to know how on earth you hit upon the lucky number."

"The Lord knows His own," replied Tassie with great gravity.

"Oh, does He? Dear me! Ah yes, of course! Good morning, Mr. Tassie!" cried Holmes, and away he hurried, fearful of laughing in the artist's face.

Describing the incident afterwards to some friends, he finished by exclaiming, "Did you ever

know anything so funny? The idea of his brag-
ging about being one of the Lord's own, and he all
the while making a collection of Priapian gems!"

As a matter of fact Tassie was noted for his
collection of this nature. The elder Tassie, a man
of real genius, made one of the largest collections
of antique gems then in existence, a complete set
of which he supplied, "by command," to Catherine,
Empress of Russia, in 1783. The Tassie collection
of "pastes in imitation of gems and cameos," designed "to represent the origin, progress, and
present state of engraving," thus made for the
great Tsarina, was arranged and described by
Rudolph Eric Raspe, a German savant, professor
of archæology and keeper of the Museum of Anti-
quities at Cassel, and the author of several important
works, including, it is said, the famous *Adventures
of Baron Munchausen*. Raspe was a man of infinite
wit and humour, and one of the quaintest of university stories, told in verse, and still recited by German
students at their convivial gatherings, is attributed
to his pen. It records how a very green Black
Forest youth, on his arrival at the university, was
taken hold of by a student named Hans Schrecke,
and carefully schooled as to how he should answer
certain questions which would, on his presentation
to the professor of divinity, be put to him by that

worthy. This schooling was combined with certain duties paid to twelve goblets that stood on the mantle-shelf of a little tavern frequented by the students, and known as the Twelve Apostles. Each one was of different material, glass, pewter, and so forth up to gold, and each was supposed to represent in a measure the character of the apostle for whom it stood. From each likewise was imbibed a different liquor, which was reputed to inspire the devotee with the qualities of the respective saints whose names the goblets bore. The simple freshman, eager to enter upon his divinity course, drank in the teaching of the friendly and insinuating Hans, with the avidity of one whose whole nature is athirst for knowledge, and speedily went from the glass and pewter to the gold, with the result that he presently felt a fervour swelling his breast combined of the qualities of all the apostles. In due course he came before the professor of divinity, and answered his questions relative to the apostles with such readiness and discrimination—not to say elevation—that the worthy professor, taking his pipe from his mouth, murmured his approval in the words, "You are a most ready student, and of a certainty either the devil or Hans Schrecke has been your instructor!" "Ah, not the former, dear Professor," replied the student, "but the learned and genial Herr Hans

Schrecke was my noble instructor."   "I am sorry to hear it," replied the professor; "it had far better have been the devil himself.   Now go back to the tavern of the Twelve Apostles, and drink of each from the one of gold backwards, and when you come to the one of glass, drink of that twelve times, and then each day twelve times for twelve moons, and of no other."   "But, dear Professor," implored the youth, "from the goblet of glass one drinks nothing but clear water—uninspiring water!" "So be it," answered the professor; "only by so doing can you obtain the wisdom which will enable you to bear with safety the fervour and inspiration imparted by the other eleven."

CHAPTER XV

JOHN BOYDELL, the promoter of the Shakespeare Gallery, was quite a character in his day, as well as an "influence for good" in regard to art, and as such was greatly admired by Holmes, although he died when the latter was comparatively a young man, having passed away a few months before the drawing of the lottery above referred to. Still Holmes may almost be said to have been an eye-witness of the result of Boydell's energy and enterprise in making English art known and even popular on the Continent, especially that department of art with which at that time he was then perhaps most conversant, namely, engraving.

Himself an engraver by profession, Boydell soon perceived that he could do better for himself and his fellow-craftsmen by turning printseller than by plying the graver. Though he began at first with but half a shop, he did so well in that that it was not long before he had a whole one to himself. His first noteworthy enterprise was to import a large number of Vernet's "Storm," engraved by Lerpinière. But having to pay for these in money, it occurred to him that matters might be considerably improved from a business point of view if he could pay for them with English prints. He accordingly got William Woollett to engrave Wilson's "Niobe," paying him £150 for it, and at once began to export large quantities. This was followed by the "Phaeton" of the same artist (published in 1763), which had an especially large sale on the Continent. Gradually an extensive business in British engravings was developed abroad, and with the increase of his capital Boydell's enterprise was greatly stimulated, with the result that at one time or another he gave commissions to most of the leading engravers of the day. Amongst others he employed besides Woollett, were M'Cordell, Hall, Heath, Sharp, J. Smith, Valentine Green, and Earlom. A large proportion of the prints issued were after Reynolds, R. Wilson, Benjamin West, and other English painters. His foreign trade made the works of English engravers and English painters known on the Continent for the first time. The receipts from West's "Death of General Wolfe" and his "Battle of La Hogue" (both engraved by

Woollett) were almost fabulous. In 1790—the year that he was Lord Mayor of London—Boydell stated that his receipts from the " Death of General Wolfe " alone were £15,000, notwithstanding both this and other of his prints were copied by the best engravers of Paris and Vienna.

But although Boydell employed many other engravers, his chief works were done by Woollett, who was perhaps the best all-round craftsman in his department of his day. The prints of the " Niobe " were originally sold at 5s., but a fine proof has since sold for £50. His " Battle of La Hogue " is generally regarded as one of his finest works, though he was equally successful in landscape, being particularly gifted in the interpretation of moving cloud and water, as well as in the delineation of foliage. The English school of engraving was greatly raised through his exertions. He was a man of very unselfish character, and worked as much for the love of his art as for money. He spared no pains in his work, took pleasure in overcoming its difficulties, and whenever he had finished a plate went up to the roof of his house and fired off a cannon to announce and commemorate the fact. This was his cock-crow, as one of his brother-engravers put it. He lived for many years in Green Street, Leicester Fields, subsequently removing to Charlotte Street, Rathbone Place, and was well known as one of the characters of the day.

But to return to Boydell. Having accumulated a large fortune, he (in 1786) embarked upon a new and still more important enterprise in connection with art. This was to publish by subscription a series of prints illustrative of Shakespeare's plays, after pictures painted expressly for the work by English artists. All the best known and most highly reputed native artists received commissions for pictures, and when finished they were exhibited in a gallery specially erected for the purpose in Pall Mall. At the exhibition, which took place in 1789, there were 34 pictures hung. By 1791 the number of works had increased to 65, and by 1792 to 162. The total number executed was 170, many of these being in sculpture. One of the latter was the bas-relief of Banks called the " The Apotheosis of Shakespeare," which was placed over the entrance. There were also two bas-reliefs by the Hon. Mrs. Damer. The latter belonged to an old family of aristocratic connections but reduced circumstances, one scion of which signally distinguished himself. He was one of the Queen's earliest pages, and was greatly esteemed by Her Majesty for his kindly and attentive disposition. But the time came when, on account of increasing age and infirmities, the respected servitor had to be pensioned off, and someone else put in his place. It grieved the old man for a time to have to change his wonted habits, but he was consoled in some measure by being allowed to be present at certain functions, such as garden parties and the like. It was at one of these that he so greatly distinguished himself, and at the same time vastly amused his former mistress.

Attending a garden party at Buckingham Palace, he was seen wandering about alone by Her Majesty, who, ever thoughtful for her servants, and doubly so for her old and tried ones, hastened towards him with extended hand and a kindly word of greeting. He took the proffered hand and held it for a moment while he gazed with a smiling, though puzzled expression at the Queen; then he said, " I know that face—I know it as well as I know any face; but—pardon me, madame—I can't for the life of me recollect where I have seen it." " Poor Damer!" exclaimed the Queen with a smile, as she turned away, "poor Damer!" The old man looked after her for a moment and then asked a gardener who happened to pass by who the lady was that had just spoken to him. When told that it was the Queen, he laughed and said, "I'm afraid Her Majesty will think I have forgotten her!"

Boydell's Shakespeare was published in 1802,

and, as almost everyone now knows, it contained prints after paintings by Reynolds, Stothard, Romney, Northcote, Smirke, Fuseli, Opie, Barry, West, Richard Westall, Hamilton, Wright (of Derby), Angelica Kaufmann, and others. But by this time the French Revolution had put a stop to his continental trade, and placed him in such difficulties that in 1804 he was obliged to apply to Parliament for permission to dispose of his property by lottery. The result enabled him to pay off his liabilities, but he did not live long enough to see Tassie carry off the prize.

As already said, the Gallery was purchased by the British Institution, which held its exhibitions therein for upwards of half a century. The British Gallery did a great deal of good in its time, and was the resort of artists who were not in favour with the Royal Academy. On this account, perhaps, it was not greatly admired by Academicians, and one in particular, noted for his rancour, was never so delighted as when he could deal a blow against it. Possibly these ungenerous attacks were the chief reason of its having finally to close its doors. Had the artists as a body rallied to its support, this catastrophe might have been averted; but they seem to be the only set of craftsmen left who have no trade organisation, and who are destitute of any sort of *esprit de corps*—until they get into the Academy.

But the attacks from outside were not the sole cause of the Institution's downfall. Those who relied upon it for support and publicity were not always wise; sometimes they were the reverse. One instance of the latter description may be mentioned, as it points a moral, and makes besides a very good story. Inskipp was a constant exhibitor at the British Gallery. He was an artist who, though he painted figure subjects in a rough, sloppy manner, was much thought of in his day, and had the good fortune to be generally well placed at the British Institution. The Academy, however, in his later years failed to appreciate his work as he desired, and he did not get much "show" on its walls; the consequence being that he never spared that Institution when he had a chance of slinging a stone at it. On one occasion his missile proved to be a boomerang, much to his surprise. When one spring the exhibition of the British Institution was opened it was found that he had a picture there in which was a donkey on whose flank were inscribed the letters R.A. This was considered a great joke, and the laugh was against the Royal Academy until Clint, the Associate, sauntered into the Gallery, saw the ass so humorously R.A.'d, and exclaimed,

"Hallo! what's this? R.A.! Oh, I see—Rejected Associate!" This turned the tables—and, it may be added, the laugh also—so effectually upon poor Inskipp that he never got over it. Nor did the British Institution long survive it.

· But apart from these little amenities, it is a thousand pities that the Institution was allowed to come to an end. It did an immense deal in its time to foster British art, not only by the encouragement of rising men, but by its annual winter exhibitions of Old Masters; for to it is due the initiation of the movement which was afterwards so successfully taken up by the Academy.

Holmes was ever a warm friend of the British Gallery, although he never exhibited there. This did not prevent him from venting a bit of harmless satire against it now and again, as when he once observed, "If you deduct B.I. from R.A., you have the remainder XX—Xpectation and Xasperation!"

But though the artist had doubtless many faults, they were never of the heart. Friends were the same to him whether they were rich or poor, one might almost say, wise or foolish. Misfortune never alienated him or checked the flow of his sympathies. One old friend, who in his later years fell into much trouble, received both sympathy and aid from him, as well as gave him much amusement. This was a man named Tickle, who, after trying many occupations, went finally into the coal trade and soon found himself in the debtors' prison, a bankrupt.

Holmes visited him there, and in the course of conversation asked him what made him become a coal dealer.

" I weally dotht know," replied Tickle, who had a terrible lisp. "It wath altogether a black bithneth."

He attributed his failures generally, however, to a termagant of a wife. In condoling with his friend on this infliction, Holmes remarked that anyway it was better to have a woman with a violent temper than a sulky one. "The storm is fierce while it lasts, but it is soon over," he added.

"Oh, the ithn't thulky," replied Tickle, "the's pathionate—exthwemely pathionate—and a pathionate woman can do more miththief in five minuteth than a thulky one can do in a lifetime."

Holmes certainly had the knack of making acquaintance with the oddest sort of people, and of extracting the greatest amount of amusement out of them.

Another of his friends was Lord Templeton, who was a well-known character in his day, always to be seen driving furiously about in a light cabriolet with his hat on the back of his head. He took a fancy to a pretty girl who sat to the artist for "Trulla" in *Hudibras*, and for female characters in several other of his subject pictures painted for Mr. Taylor of Strensham. The girl's mother was as ugly as she herself was pretty, and when Templeton one day dropped in while both were in the studio, Holmes, seeing his lordship glance once or twice at the elder, and always ready to help along a little fun, introduced her as the mother of his model. "What! what!" exclaimed Templeton, looking first at one and then at the other, the mother making absurd "bobs" the while. "What! You the mother of that pretty girl, and you so—you so—— Impossible!" He finished up with a loud laugh, the artist joining in.

"It was very rude," remarked Holmes drily, describing the scene; "but it was impossible to help it, the old woman looked so absurd bobbing up and down and grinning. And then the Witch of Endor was a beauty in comparison with her."

The girl afterwards married — well, it was thought, and she was lost sight of for a time. Then one of Holmes's sons met her aunt and asked after her. "Oh, she is married," the woman replied. "Indeed! who has she married?" "An *itinerary* surgeon; I forget his other name," was the reply.

But the "itinerary" appears to have tired of his bargain after a while, and went off to America, leaving his wife with two or three children. · Lord Templeton then came to the aid of the family, putting them into a tobacconist's shop, but dropping them after a time, like the husband, as too expensive a luxury.

Among the more intellectual of the artist's many acquaintance was the famous Robert Owen, the Socialist. They first met at the house of a gentleman who was a relative of Owen's. The latter was at that time a young man, and not so widely known as he afterwards became. On this account it was perhaps that the artist had not previously heard of him or his views. He then spoke of his colonies as "Parallelograms," a name which greatly amused Holmes, who, though not much taken by the idealist's schemes, was greatly impressed by the intelligence and the fine enthusiasm of the man.

After this they did not see each other again for several years. Their second meeting took place on the occasion of a lecture delivered by Owen in the Egyptian Hall. Holmes then renewed his acquaintance, and Owen became a frequent visitor at 15 Wilton Street. He was there introduced to Mr. and Mrs. Hurlstone, and was invited by them to 9 Chester Street. Hurlstone painted an excellent portrait of him, the present whereabouts of which it would be pleasing to know.

Owen was not a popular man with society. His religious views, and more particularly his advanced ideas in regard to matrimony and divorce (divorce at that time being almost impossible, even to the richest), put him outside "the dining and being dined" class of society. Holmes, though a warm friend of reform and in some respects an idealist, found little in Owen's schemes to commend itself to his sober common-sense. The man's enthusiasm for humanity he admired, and believed many of his ideas, if properly carried out, would greatly benefit society ; but, strangely enough, it was not the idealistic tendency of Owen's general schemes so much as their dry utilitarianism that was most repugnant to him, as well as to Hurlstone. In many respects his ideas were very crude. His views of life had been gathered from the lower walks of life, and were of the simplest. They did not extend much beyond the physical wants, and how best to supply them. Believing that four hours' work a day was sufficient to provide for a man's animal needs, he would have had every man labour for that length of time, and devote the remainder of the day to recreation and study.

But his opinions changed somewhat after this

second acquaintance with Holmes. At the latter's table, as well as at Hurlstone's, he met a different set of people from those he had been used to, but chiefly artists, writers, wits, and perhaps one would add at the present day, "cranks"; and the enlarged views of society he there obtained caused him to extend or modify many of his notions. The change was noticed in his lectures. For one thing, he had not previously realised any of the higher wants such as are satisfied by the study of art, science, or literature, and only now began to consider in what way they might be made useful in his "parallelogrammatic" system.

Holmes, with his penchant for looking at things in a ludicrous light, once suggested a difficulty in regard to the partition of work, saying that he himself might object to sweeping chimneys, or other such *discolouring* work. Owen promptly got over the difficulty with the remark, "Oh, the boys would do all that kind of work. They like to be in the dirt."

Another answer he gave to an objection showed how, in his cut-and-dried system, the facts of human nature were quite got rid of. Someone observed that a Napoleon might arise when he had reorganised society according to his plan, and knock his parallelograms into a cocked hat. "Oh no," said he. "Education would have entirely changed the thoughts of men, rendering each one amenable to the others and to the general order."

On one occasion there was a great Socialist gathering at Highbury Barn, to which Holmes and his family, Hurlstone and his wife, and others of their set went, "for the fun of the thing." There was the usual discoursing, eating and drinking, and the like, the whole finishing up with a dance. Owen, who was tall and of manly proportions, with strongly-marked features, yet with an expression and a manner as gentle and simple as a child, walked about smiling and benignant, chatting first with one and then with another, and looking, with his grand head, as one man remarked, "like a deity."

An amusing little incident occurred, showing how little easy it is to bring human nature down to a common level. When the music was going, and the couples were whirling about the room to its inspiring strains, a little man approached Mrs. Hurlstone, and asked her if she would favour him with her hand in a dance. She immediately drew herself up and rather haughtily refused; whereupon the man replied with a grin, "You're not very *Socialist*." "Oh, I quite forgot where we are!" she exclaimed, turning to Holmes. "It will take an age to socialise you, I'm afraid," he returned with a laugh. "Here, let me give you a lesson in parallelogramisation," and away he went round the room with a hastily - picked companion of the working-class type, with whom he soon floundered against the benignantly-smiling Mr. Owen.

"Ah, this is nice of you, Mr. Holmes—this is very nice! We are progressing beautifully. At this rate we shall soon reach the—soon reach the——" "Millennium," suggested the artist with a laugh, and away he whirled again with his partner.

Recounting the joke afterwards to Hurlstone, and observing Mrs. Hurlstone's smile, Holmes remarked, "You probably, Mrs. Hurlstone, would think the progress was towards a Mile-end-ium?" But she did not see the point of the witticism.

Another of the artist's reminiscences of Owen, though touching his views on religious subjects, may be recorded without irreverence. At the close of his lectures in the Egyptian Hall it was customary to give an opportunity for questions to be asked and objections advanced. One evening a clergyman rose, but instead of attempting to combat the lecturer's position, he simply held up a Bible and said, "This is my stronghold; I believe in this; on this I am prepared to stand or fall." "Have you any argument to advance, sir?" politely asked Mr.

Owen.   No, he had simply to say that in the Scriptures he had the most implicit belief. "Can you believe that these three candles are one?" questioned the lecturer. "Yes, certainly," replied the clergyman. "That being so," returned Mr. Owen with a bow, "I have nothing more to say; there is indeed nothing to be said."

Towards the close of his days Owen became a convert to Spiritualism, and everybody said, repeating the witticism of one man, that in the end the best of china got cracked. To which Holmes's answer was, "The point that they do not see is that the crack was there from the beginning."

CHAPTER XVI

ANOTHER of Holmes's most intimate friends, and a man who was sufficiently notorious, if not celebrated, in his day, calls for a few paragraphs if only for the misfortunes that embittered his days and finally brought his career to a tragic end.   Many, possibly, whose memories carry them back to the mid-period of the century will recall the name of the Baron de Bode and the oft-repeated story of his claims upon the British Government, or, to put it more correctly, upon the Crown, consequent upon his being obliged to take refuge in England during the Reign of Terror.

Baron Clement Joseph Philip Pen de Bode was the eldest son of Charles Augustus de Bode, the first Baron, a German by birth, and was born at Loxley Park, in the county of Stafford, in 1777, his mother being a daughter of Mr. Kinnersley of that place.   Baron Charles Augustus acquired an estate at Soultz in Alsace in 1787, and made it over to his son in 1791. He migrated in 1793 and died four years later. The son went to reside in Alsace in 1787, and migrated with his father in 1793, whereupon the estates at Soultz were confiscated. Subsequently he became a naturalised British subject.

Thus matters stood when, upon the downfall of Napoleon, Louis the Eighteenth was raised to the throne of France, and a treaty of peace was signed between that Power and England in May 1814. In the following year (November 1815) a convention was framed in accordance with the above treaty, whereby it was agreed that a commission should be formed, composed of one half English and the other half French commissioners, for the purpose of examining the claims of British subjects and determining the amount of indemnity they should receive for the loss of property in France in consequence of and during the Revolution, and a sum of money or property representing a capital of 70,000,000 francs, bearing interest at 5 per cent, was at the same time set aside to pay the said claims.

The Baron first of all sent in his claim to the French commissioners, but being informed that he must lay it before the English section of the commission, he rectified his error and presented his claim for indemnity in 1816, within the limit of time fixed for such demands to be deposited. Many of the claims were paid, but the Baron de Bode's was passed over. Subsequently a change was made in the commission, the French section of it being done away with, and a lump sum, amounting to something like £2,000,000 sterling, being paid over to the British Government with which to settle all outstanding claims.

Again and again the Baron applied to the commission for payment of his indemnity, producing all the documents necessary to support his claim, and proving his title up to the hilt, but still without success. Finally, in 1822 the commission decided against him. The matter was then brought before the Privy Council, who upheld the decision of the commission. Some years later (May 1826) the case came before the House of Commons on petition, and once, if not twice, subsequently, but on each occasion with the same result—non-success.

But the Baron was not to be beaten, and in 1837 or 1838 he entered an action-at-law against the Crown, or, in legal phraseology, instituted a petition of right. This was only the first of a series of trials, the upshot result of which was that, though De Bode won verdict after verdict, he never got one step nearer to the realisation of his claim. In the end the disappointment consequent upon these repeated failures broke his heart.

Holmes used often to speak of the visit De Bode paid him the day the jury gave a verdict in his favour, and found him entitled to a sum of £350,000. As he entered the studio he exclaimed—

"*Enfin, mon cher ami—enfin j'ai triomphé!* Justice has been done me at last—I am to have £350,000, *Enfin—mais comme je suis las!*"

De Bode was then getting old, but the worries and anxieties he had gone through had aged him more than his actual years. When he said he was tired, Holmes noted the deep furrows that care had ploughed upon his face and the shadow of sorrow it had cast over his eyes, and he could hardly contain his grief.

" But you do not congratulate me on my success, *mon cher Monsieur Holmes*," said the Baron.

" I congratulate you with all my heart," the artist replied, "but I shall be able to congratulate you with much more heartiness when you get your money."

De Bode was struck with his friend's words, and asked, " But shall I not get my money now ? Will they not pay it to me ?"

" Who ? "

" The Government."

Holmes shook his head.

"You afflict me," said De Bode. "Do you think they will not pay me?"

"I think, my dear Baron, that you have still to get your money, and I do not exactly see who is going to pay you."

The artist had lived through a bad time; he had mixed with all ranks of society, and had seen how corrupt and rotten it was. He was not at heart what would be called a cynical man, but what he had seen of governments had made him doubt; and he did not believe the litigant was any nearer the actual accomplishment of justice than before his verdict.

De Bode went away saying that if the money were not paid him he should sue the Queen. This eventually he did. The case was tried before Lord Denman, who, to his eternal disgrace be it said, found that, though De Bode's claim was good, and the verdict of the jury just, yet he had no means of recovery, as the persons who had received the money and who ought to have paid it were all dead. A more unfair judgment was probably never given in a court of law.

Our system of jurisprudence has been improved since then, and it is to be hoped that never again will it be possible for an English judge to fail in regard to so elementary a principle of justice as that the responsibility of governments continues notwithstanding the decease of individuals, as did Denman. Nevertheless, our system of so-called justice is very far from perfect. It is one by which a suitor is apt to get a monstrous deal of law, but very little equity.

This terrible end to the poor Baron's long years of effort proved too much for him, and he was a little while afterwards found dead in his bed.[1]

An inquest was held, and as the facts of his life and of his sad end were brought out, the jury found that the deceased gentleman had died from natural causes, but that his death had been accelerated by the bad treatment of the Government. The coroner refused to receive this verdict. " It means a charge of manslaughter against the Government," he said. " You must retire again and reconsider your verdict, gentlemen." And like true invertebrate British jurymen, they did as they were told, and spared the Government.

De Bode left a son, who continued to prosecute the family claim against the Crown, though with the same ill success as his father. The last time it was heard of was in 1853, when Lord Lyndhurst brought the matter before the House of Lords, and in a speech that did credit alike to his manhood

---

[1] This took place in 1846.

and the high reputation he had won as a lawyer, laid bare the flagrant injustice that had been done in the case of this long-pending claim. But all his eloquence was in vain; the money had been swallowed up by " Bode Palace," [1] or in some other way, and there was no redress.

It is worth while, however, quoting two or three sentences from Lord Lyndhurst's speech to show the light in which such an authority viewed the matter :—

" I have, my Lords," he said, "grown gray in the profession of the law, but I have never in my experience known a question so completely mystified, if I may so express myself, by the perverted ingenuity of its practitioners, as this unfortunate question respecting the claim of the Baron de Bode." He further said, " I must add that I never in my experience witnessed a more inexcusable and flagrant breach of trust than that which has been thus committed. . . . Every step has been marked with low chicanery and technical obstruction."

De Bode was well known amongst the aristocracy, by whom he was greatly esteemed for the courageous way in which he bore his misfortunes, as well as for his cheery good-nature and light-

---

[1] This was the name given by De Bode to Buckingham Palace, which, as he used to say, had been built with his money.

heartedness under crosses that would have soured ninety-nine men out of every hundred. By these friends he was largely supported during his protracted litigations through gifts and loans. One of his best and most generous patrons, to whom he was introduced by Holmes, was Sir Gerald Noël, afterwards the Earl of Gainsborough, and father of the Rev. Baptist Noël, the famous preacher.

Holmes never spoke of this nobleman except in terms of the highest praise, as being the most admirable type of a man that he had ever known. He had many anecdotes of his kindness and generosity, as well as of his invariable good-humour and sunshiny nature. It appears that as a young man he joined some bank speculation, and when it unfortunately failed, he was so seriously involved—there being then no such thing as limited liability—that he had practically to give up his estates to the liquidators and live upon an allowance out of them. This meant greatly narrowed means for years; nevertheless Sir Gerald bore his altered circumstances, with their constant need for careful retrenchment, without a murmur. Nay, he even managed at times to be generous in the midst of his poverty.

Thus, on one occasion, when a new church was to

be built in his neighbourhood, and the subscription list was going round, those who had the management of it thoughtfully refrained from laying it before the baronet until the larger donors had been passed, and they had come down to the givers of £50 and under, delicately suggesting, of course, that they could not expect him in his impoverished condition to give more. Sir Gerald took the list and carefully ran his eye down it, noting the various donors, from those whose names stood first to sums of £500 and the like, and so on to the end, and then, taking a pen, put down his signature to a sum of £1000.

CHAPTER XVII

ARISTOCRATIC FRIENDS AND PATRONS

AMONGST the artist's aristocratic friends there were few so generous in their support and patronage as Mrs. .Essex Cholmondeley, the sister of Lord Delamere. His friendship with this lady and her family continued for many years, and he was frequently both at Cassia, her residence, and at Vale Royal, the seat of Lord Delamere, and painted portraits of many of the family. The following letters all refer to portrait commissions ; but they have a general interest apart from that circumstance :—

VALE ROYAL, *August* 9, 1835.

SIR—I am desired by Lord and Lady Delamere to hope that it will not be inconvenient to you to come to Vale Royal as soon as possible, as the youngest boy is very soon going to school, and the second son, being in the army, may be called away any moment. If you will write to me and fix any day that you will be at Vale Royal, Lady Delamere will send the pony carriage to meet you at Northwich.

ESSEX CHOLMONDELEY.

Please to direct to me, Mrs. Essex Cholmondeley, under cover to Lord Delamère, Vale Royal, Northwich, Cheshire.

P.S.—The parents of the youths wish their likenesses to be taken in water colours, the same as the young Cholmondeleys of Hodnet Hall, and not in oils.

3 SUMMER SEAT, BOOTLE, LIVERPOOL.

SIR—It will much oblige me if you will undertake a journey to Knutsford in Cheshire. I wish for my brother Charles's picture as a small full-length painting. He is a very elderly gentleman and not so fine a figure as my eldest brother, but was thought handsome in his youth. I have apprized him of your approach, and his very oldest coat has now been brushed. Pray allow me some interest in your truly elegant likenesses. Vale Royal will receive you from Knutsford, and I entreat you to follow its master and gain a likeness of him.—From your true friend, ESSEX CHOLMONDELEY.

Charles Cholmondeley and his daughters will mention you at Tatton and Dunham Massey, two principal mansions in Cheshire. Tatton possesses a numerous family, and the high-bred manners at Dunham Massey will, I am sure, be approved of by you.

September 29, 1835.

CASSIA, *May* 29, 1836.

SIR—I hope you are taking my niece Miss Drummond's likeness—you are so superior an artist. She is rather fat, but pretty, with elegant hands and feet; she lives at Chesham Place, Grosvenor Place, and will expect you, if you have not already called upon her. Her brother, John Drummond, tells me he will be happy to see you, and I desire you will take a likeness of Miss Hester Drummond, his daughter. They must be done in the style of Charley Cholmondeley's, and when finished you must send the account to me and I shall be happy to settle it. Lady

Delamere will bring the drawings to Vale Royal when she leaves London.—I am ever your true friend,

Essex Cholmondeley.

June 21, 1836.

Sir—Whenever you are at leisure I know you will oblige me in making a good likeness of a sister I never can forget, namely, Hester Drummond Conce Cholmondeley. You are expected to occupy a room in Vale Royal, where a picture hangs of her by Monsieur Monier, a French artist. You must know she was in a deep consumption when the painter drew it. Pray, I beseech you, enliven the lovely beauty, and in one of your small lengths try to recollect and represent to the eyes every beauty of body and mind in the representation of Hester Cholmondeley.—Yours much obligéd,   Essex Cholmondeley.

Cassia, *December* 20, 1837.

Sir—Surely it is encroaching on your time to write to me from Acton Park your obliging attentions. I hope you will recollect that old Mr. Okell of Sandiway is dead, and that I will accept from memory a likeness of him from you. I would not mention his demise in my last troublesome letter to you, although I thought of it. Is it possible to forget a real friend? Thank you for complying with my requests, and allow me to wish you and all your family a merry Christmas.

Essex Cholmondeley.

Cassia, 10*th March* 1839.

Sir—When you have elegantized with your pencil Archbishop Drummond and George James Cholmondeley, you will be so obliging as to introduce them at Charing Cross, for £10 each, by Essex Cholmondeley's orders. You will receive Hester and Essex Cholmondeley to copy for my nephew John Drummond, and present them to him at the same order. Take care this accompanies your beautiful effects and produce it to them, namely, to the Messrs. Drummond.

I thank Mrs. Holmes for her obliging attentions to

ESSEX CHOLMONDELEY.

CASSIA, *February* 16, 1840.

SIR—I have just received your obliging letter. I have heard from Mrs. Cholmondeley, and she agrees with me in regard to your going to Hodnet in the autumn. I hope to meet you there, but that is uncertain.

I will accept with pleasure your likeness of Reginald, as you appear to wish it.

Pray excuse this concise letter, and believe me your true friend, ESSEX CHOLMONDELEY.

Another family for whom Holmes painted almost as many portraits as for the Cholmondeleys and Delameres was that of the Duke of Leeds. The Duchess was one of his warmest and most constant friends, and he executed a miniature portrait of her as well as of the Duke. He also painted a miniature of their daughter, the beautiful Lady Charlotte Mary Lane-Fox, wife of Sackville Walter Lane-Fox, M.P., who died at a comparatively early age 17th January 1836. The following interesting letter, addressed to her aunt, has reference to the portrait in question :—

HORNBY CASTLE, *Thursday.*

MY DEAR AUNT—Thank you ten thousand times for all your news. I do hope the *aspect* is brightening and Sir R(obert) P(eel) is determined to go on as long as the King will keep him.

I am sending this by a box going up, and I seize the opportunity to enclose some hints for *Le petit Peintre au sujet de mon Portrait.* I am *si reconnaissant* for what you tell me, and shall be further obliged if you will see to the finishing. I wish the little man would scrawl in pencil on any scrap of paper the outline and how he has put the figure together, as neither the hands nor the arrangement of the flower-vase was at all defined when I last saw it.

I beg by all means the point lace may be dabbled a point higher on the shoulder. Pray see to this propriety, *je t'en prie,* dear aunt. Then the rose ; I would wish white (House of York). I did not wish the blue lining ; my conceit was to have been a sable bordure along the edge of the mantilla about the width of a boa. He will say the contrast would not be enough with the *feuille morte.* To set against this, show him a sketch of the most perfect picture in the world as to colouring, subject, " La Maîtresse de Titian," the original in the Studio Gallery at Naples ! and the colour of the squirrel, which would be nearly that of the fur. I wish not quite so red brown, and it harmonizes perfectly with the *feuille-morte* garb. I trouble your patience still further with two prints, the one of Lady Radstock, to show him the sort of balustrade and creeping plants about it, and the Duchess of Bedford, to show him the size and description of vase, which should be filled with roses, white and red. But pray tell him the red roses ought to be a tender pink, or else they make the picture look dauby and bad, and jessamine besides, if he pleases.

If he attends to these suggestions, he has our free permission to hang me (I hope the simile ends there) in the exhibition if he wishes it so much. I do not write to him, as I have troubled you with these observations, which perhaps you will at your leisure read to him. If the blue lining to my mantilla is persevered in, I beg it may be distinctly turquoise blue, or a very bright royal blue. This colour, and not a gray or Marie Louise blue for the world !

I am writing this in flying haste for the box.

I am afraid all this will be such a plague to you.—Believe me, my dear aunt, your affectionate grateful niece,   C. M. L. F.

The following letters from the Duchess of Leeds have reference to her bereavement through the death of her daughter :—

The Duchess of Leeds' compts. to Mr. Holmes, and would be very glad to see him here, and should her life extend to another year, hopes some good chance may occur to the causing his coming into the North, and that it may suit better than at present his coming to this melancholy abode. The next month the Duke will be wholly engaged with his agent's accounts, and therefore he would not desire any one else here. She need not say how very much she would like to see the sketch he writes he had done for himself, of " the head finished and the rest touched delicately." *She absolutely yearns for it*, for now that she has given Mr. Fox the miniature she never sees it ; perhaps he would have the goodness to send it here, and she would on his return to town send him the MS. book she wishes him to put a likeness into of the dear angel.

The picture must not come from his possession at present, she imagines, for she never can speak to Mr. Fox on the subject. When he and the Duke are next in town they will determine regarding all the pictures, and the Duke will give the finishing sittings for his picture.

She hopes Mr. Holmes can send her the *sketch as immediately as possible*.

Hornby Castle, *October* 28.

Begs, if Mr. Holmes can let her possess the sketch, that he will state its price.

The Duchess of Leeds is very wishful Mr. Holmes could paint her another miniature as faithful a likeness as the last of the beloved daughter, as she has given that one to Mr. Fox and cannot do without one for the dear children, and she will send him a book to town next week. She wishes him to make a sketch in water colour, as she will point out; but wishes immediately to bespeak the miniature to be doing. Is glad to say the dear children are well, so is Mr. Fox. As to herself, her malady keeps increasing.

She hopes Mr. Holmes and family are well.

HORNBY CASTLE, CATTENIK, *October* 26.

Mr. Holmes paid several visits to Hornby Castle, the Yorkshire seat of the Duke of Leeds.

Another house at which he was a frequent visitor was Woburn Abbey, the Bedfordshire seat of the Duke of Bedford. The Duchess was his very good friend, and his visits were continued after the death of the Duke. He used to say laughingly that he went to keep the place warm for Sir Edwin Land-seer, who afterwards became very intimate with the Duchess, and had, as is well known, some hopes of marrying her.

Holmes did not know the famous animal painter well, although he had met him from time to time. There is an amusing anecdote about him which is well worth relating. Once when he had gone into a new house with a garden (in St. John's Wood, I believe) he planted the latter with a lot of standard rose-trees. They did not thrive, however, and so disappointed was the artist when he was about to have a party that he bought a large quantity of paper roses and made his garden bloom resplendently with them (on his standards). He used to smile when he related the incident, because he said none of his guests detected the deception, while many praised the beauty of his garden.

Sir Josiah Mason, the Birmingham millionaire (to whom the queen-city of the Midlands owes her Erdington Orphanage and the Mason College), used to boast of a similar, though less innocent deception. At his grand dinners he was wont to put home-made gooseberry wine upon the table in place of champagne, and then laugh in his sleeve at the way his guests gulped down the liquid and praised the excellence of the vintage.

CHAPTER XVIII

THE END

HITHERTO Holmes had found life very pleasant, and upon the whole he had had no great reason to complain of want of success. But he was now destined to meet with a sore trial. Always of a perfectly honest and truthful nature himself, it did not enter into his thoughts to regard his friends as in any respect less trustworthy. Amongst the number of his business acquaintance was the head of a well-known firm of builders in Doughty Street. This man he had known since the early days of his settlement in Cirencester Place, when he had built a studio for him at the back of his house. The artist employed him also to put up a studio in Wilton Street, when he removed thither in 1828, and was charged what he considered an exorbitant price for it.

About, or shortly before, the time of removal to Wilton Street, Holmes introduced this man to his friend Mr. Taylor, of Worcester, who was meditating building upon his magnificent estate of Strensham Court, near that city, and was the means of his securing a commission that amounted in all to nearly £50,000. For this friendly service he not only barely received the thanks of the builder, but was induced by him, by the most specious pretences, to become security for a large amount. The firm, falling into difficulties shortly afterwards, realised on the artist's security, and then became bankrupt. The result may be imagined. Lawyers on both sides went to work, and when they had finished—Holmes at least was a ruined man : ruined, but neither broken nor embittered.

This was in 1846, consequently when the artist was just upon seventy years of age, and no longer capable of doing the amount or the quality of work he had formerly done. He was obliged to give up his house in Wilton Street (in 1847) and remove to humbler quarters at Hendon, where he remained for several years.

For the Mr. Taylor above mentioned he executed many commissions. Mr. Taylor was a member of the family of bankers of Worcester, but, being of a literary turn, was not employed in the business. He devoted much time and money to doing honour to the memory of Samuel Butler, the author of *Hudibras*, who was born at Strensham. To him the village owes a memorial of the poet; by him also Holmes was commissioned to paint several pictures the subjects of which were taken from Butler's famous poem. One of them represented the widow visiting Hudibras in the stocks. Doubtless some, if not the whole, of these pictures still adorn the walls of Strensham Court.

In 1853 the artist lost his wife. She died on the day that their eldest surviving son Henry landed in Melbourne. This son was the cause of considerable grief to his father in his latter years. He was attracted to Australia during the great gold rush, but does not appear to have gained much from the change save disappointment. He engaged in some theatrical enterprises, married an actress, and after condign failure, migrated with his family to Auckland, New Zealand, where he became scenic artist at the Opera House, and where he died of suffocation, in consequence of a fire in his workshop, on the 24th of January 1885.

Soon after his arrival in the queen-city of the Antipodes Mr. Henry Holmes ceased to write home, and from then until his death his family had no communication whatever from him. This neglect to acquaint them with his whereabouts and fortunes was the cause of much trouble to his father, who had always evinced a tender solicitude for the welfare of his children. But, despite his grief, he could not help laughing very heartily at a droll saying of Hurlstone's once when he had asked if any news had been received from Harry. "No," said Holmes sadly. "Oh well, never mind!" replied Hurlstone. "If you have not heard, depend upon it he is making his fortune."

After the death of his wife Holmes's time for some years was divided between London and Shropshire and the adjoining counties, where he had many friends and where he spent much of his time going from one house to another. Amongst the number of his warmest friends were Viscount Hill, of Hawkstone (where Rowland Hill was born); the Corbets of Acton Reynold; the Kenyons of Pradoe, near Shrewsbury; Viscountess Dungannon, and many others. In not a few of these houses a room was constantly kept in readiness for him, and he always had a hearty welcome when he paid their owners a visit.

Nor, when speaking of his friends, should the Misses Perceval, of Ealing, the daughters of Spencer Perceval, the murdered Premier, be forgotten. These three ladies were always very sincere and devoted friends of the artist. It was under their roof that he first made the acquaintance of Walpole, who found in his unfailing good spirits so striking a contrast to his own more serious mood.

When in London he lived with his sons Edward and George, the former of whom had succeeded to a good deal of his father's practice as a portrait-painter. These were now the only members of his family remaining to him.

The last four or five years of his life he spent entirely in London, invariably active and cheerful, albeit mildly regretting the advances and ravages of old age. "This is that confounded old age," he would say when he felt the touch of rheumatism stiffening his fingers and so preventing him from playing the flute so deftly as of yore. "It is that confounded old age stealing upon one in the dark. *Eh bien, telle est la vie!*"

This latter was a favourite saying of his, and seemed to sum up in a convenient phrase his philosophy of life, which was simply to make the most of it by contentment and good-humour. That had always been his way, and on the whole he had enjoyed life. Perhaps it would have been better for him in the end, and for those he left behind him, if he had taken more care of his means. He appeared to think so himself in his later days, but the thought was not allowed to trouble him much. When speaking of his inability to leave anything for his sons, he would say—

"Oh well, I had to fight my way and do

the best I could; you will have to do the same."

Then he would add, "There's a lot of enjoyment to be got out of life, even by a poor man, if he knows how to go about it"—or words to that effect.

Though, like everything else in the world, it has its drawbacks, this way of looking at life is not without its advantages, and Holmes did not choose it altogether without thought. Amongst others he had seen his friend Hurlstone grow to care more and more for money, and to worry himself about many things, until he became half insane; and though he left a competency to each of his sons, they profited little, if at all, by it. Thus he came to think that a profession, a love of work, courage, and contentment were about the best equipment for the battle of life that anyone could have. They had served him very well, and he thought they would do the same for his sons. "Work hard and never mind," he used to say to people when they were worrying too much. "Life is ever the same; you can't cure it of its sorrow by caring, therefore do not care too much, but do your work—and play the flute when you can." This generally came at the end with a little laugh. Flute-playing to him signified a sensible way of taking recreation.

Such had been his way of looking at life all

through his career, and it had robbed it of much of its harshness and many of its minor worries. Thus he performed upon his flute—his early friend—up to within a week or two of his death, and found in it, and in his art, a never-failing source of consolation and delight.

Sitting one winter evening by the fire, shortly before the end, with one of his sons, and the latter having spoken a little despondingly of life, for death had again been busy, he said, "It is no good looking on the dark side. If you do that you will always see enough to make life sad, and to depress and discourage you. Look on the bright side; it is much the best way. You will then generally find enough to keep you cheerful and in good spirits most of the time. But, above all, seek for strength and comfort in your art. I have seen life in all its phases, and have had my ups and downs; but remember when I am gone that there has at all times been but one real and lasting pleasure to me, and that has been the study and practice of my art."

Not long after this, in the eighty-third year of his age, he quietly passed away in his sleep. As his life had been, for the most part, happy and tranquil, so was his death. About a fortnight previously he had spent the evening with some young friends, and was as gay and almost as frolicsome as the rest.

He stayed out rather late and caught a slight cold. For several days no alarm was felt, but two days before his death it took a serious turn, and his strength fell away with amazing rapidity. Still he kept up, and the very last day of his life he went out and took a short walk. Going to bed rather late, he fell into a doze, and in that state passed away. He retained the full use of all his faculties to the last, including his eyesight, which was hardly in the least impaired. The date of his death was the 24th of February 1860.

JOHN VARLEY

CHAPTER I

IT is given to but few men to fail so utterly in respect to everything relating to worldly affairs, and yet to leave such a name behind both for goodness of heart and for the sterling results of genius, as did John Varley, the artist, and one of the founders of the Society of Painters in Water Colours. Born only three years after Turner, and five before David Cox, he came into the world at a time when the national art of water-colour painting was still in its infancy, and as yet giving but slight indication of the sturdy growth to which it was shortly to attain, and to attain in large measure through his example and guidance.

His father, Richard Varley, was a native of Epworth, in Lincolnshire, famous as the birthplace of John Wesley; but, not finding sufficient scope for his talents and energy in that place, he removed into Yorkshire, where he married, his wife being a

Fleetwood, a descendant of General Fleetwood, some time Lord Deputy of Ireland, who married Cromwell's daughter Bridget. Thus, through his mother, John Varley inherited the blood both of the Cromwells and the Fleetwoods.

Richard Varley did not find Yorkshire any more to his taste than Lincolnshire, and he accordingly soon migrated to London, where his son John was born. This event took place on the 17th of August 1778, at Hackney, in what was previously the Blue Posts Tavern, but which, with its surrounding grounds, his father had converted into a private residence. It stood next to the churchyard, and seems to have been a pleasant and sufficiently commodious abode.

We have no means now of ascertaining precisely what was Richard Varley's calling. That he was a man of some mechanical ability and of considerable scientific attainments there can be no doubt. It has generally been understood that he was for some time tutor to the famous Earl of Stanhope, but doubt has recently been thrown upon this supposition, the suggestion being that his elder brother Samuel was the one who held that position. Such could hardly have been the case, however ; for at the time of Richard Varley's decease the former was a thriving watchmaker and jeweller, a position he could not have attained all at once. It is more than probable that Richard was originally of the same profession as his brother, and that he gave it up for the more intellectual, and very likely at the same time more lucrative, one of tutor. At all events John Varley appears always to have asserted that his father was tutor to the son of Earl Stanhope, father of the celebrated Lady Hester Stanhope, who acted for some time as secretary to her uncle Pitt, but after his death went to Syria, where she assumed the male dress of a native of that country, and devoted herself to the study of astrology.

It is not a matter of merely recent observation how deeply the opinions of a man of original mind may pervade and influence his surroundings, and there is no telling but the character of Earl Stanhope may, through his father, have had its effect upon the subject of this biography. Charles Stanhope (who succeeded his father in the peerage in 1786) distinguished himself by espousing the principles of the French Revolution, which he carried out to the extent of setting aside the titles and privileges of a peer. He was elected a member of the Royal Society in 1772, and devoted a large portion of his income to experiments in science and philosophy, which resulted in a number of valuable inventions. Amongst others were a method of securing buildings from fire (which, however, proved impracticable), the printing press and the lens which bear his name, and a monochord for tuning musical instruments. He also suggested improvements in canal locks, made improvements in steam navigation (1795-97), and contrived two calculating machines. His experiments in electricity resulted in the publication of a volume on the Principles of Electricity. Indeed, so devoted was Earl Stanhope to his scientific and literary pursuits that he neglected his wife and children for them. His youngest daughter, Lady Lucy Rachel Stanhope, eloped with an apothecary of Sevenoaks, who used to serve the family, and her father, notwithstanding his republican principles, never forgave her for the *mésalliance*.

It may have been the example of Earl Stanhope, who would naturally be much talked about in his father's family, that subsequently caused John Varley to turn his attention to invention, and perhaps to speculative science generally.

John was one of a family of five, three boys and two girls, all born at the house in Hackney. After John came Cornelius, and then William Fleetwood, both of whom, as we shall see, like their elder brother, made their mark as artists, as did also one of the girls, Elizabeth, who became the wife of William Mulready, the Academician.

John almost from his infancy found more delight in drawing than in any other amusement. He was noted among his schoolfellows not only for the possession of this gift, but also for a degree of muscular strength which exceeded that of all the lads of his age with whom he associated. The latter qualification was the means of bringing him frequently into hot water, for he could never see a boy put upon or in any way molested by another without interfering. Many were the times that he felt himself thus called upon to intervene in the cause of justice. Of so generous and amiable a disposition was he, indeed, and so full of courage, that he would never think twice when there seemed need for his assistance, but would at once take sides with the oppressed, even though his antagonist were a much older or bigger lad than himself. The consequence was that in a short time there was hardly a youth in the neighbourhood who would fight him alone. Once, we are told, when upon some trifling occasion which produced a quarrel three attacked him at once, he maintained the unequal contest for several minutes and objected to any interference, till the onlookers stepped in and insisted on fair play. He then fought his three antagonists singly, and punished them all.

As he grew in years Varley's bent for art became

stronger. But in accordance with the almost in-variable rule in such cases, the disposition was discouraged—at least by his father, who would not hear of his son's becoming an artist. Painting, said the elder Varley, was a poor trade, and none of his children should become artists. But while man proposes, God disposes. At the age of thirteen John was placed with a silversmith, with the view of his serving an apprenticeship to that craft. But his father dying (November 1791) before he had reached his fourteenth year, the intention was not proceeded · with. Friends urged his mother to apprentice him to a mechanical trade, but either from inability to pay the premium required in those days, or for some other equally cogent reason, this course was not taken. Possibly it may be, as has been said, that she did not wish to go counter to her son's desire, his heart being firmly set upon becoming an artist.

There is a story, and not by any means an unlikely one, to the effect that while still a boy Varley was in the employ of a stockbroker named Trower, his duty being to sweep out the office and run errands. This gentleman, to while away the time, was in the habit of making sketches on scraps of paper, which in the end were generally thrown upon the floor. These young Varley used to collect, and afterwards try to copy them. One of these copies Mr. Trower by some chance got hold of, and found it so well done that he told the youth he had better take to drawing. It is further stated[1] that ever after this Mr. Trower and his family assisted Varley, though in what way or to what extent is not recorded.

A short time after his father's death young Varley was placed with a law stationer. His nature, however, was one that could not be tamed down to the sordid drudgery of such an occupation, and one fine morning, having emptied his pocket in the purchase of paper and pencils, with the exception of three halfpence, he set forth on his first sketching excursion. His mother saw nothing of him for several days. At length he returned dirty, half-famished, and with sketches of Hampstead and Highgate in his portfolio.

Mrs. Varley, who had more taste for art than her husband, appears at length to have been convinced that it was useless to oppose her son's inclination to art, and decided to give him every encouragement, and to assist him in his studies as much as was in her power.[2] Unfortunately, how-

---

[1] Roget, *History of the Royal Society of Painters in Water Colours.*

[2] Mrs. Varley appears to have been a woman of exemplary piety and strength of character, and thoroughly worthy of her descent from the Cromwells and the Fleetwoods.

ever, it was not much that she could do, for after her husband's death she seems to have been greatly straitened in means. The house at Hackney had to be given up; and a few years later we find John residing with his widowed mother and his brothers and sisters in a court off Old Street, City Road, opposite to St. Luke's Hospital.*

Left thus at liberty to follow his bent, Varley resolved to support himself by his pencil. It was a courageous resolution, and he went nobly to work, drawing whatever came in his way, copying figures, making sketches of animals, and exhibiting the results of his labours to his friends and acquaintance, some of whom encouraged him to renewed perseverance by an occasional purchase. His drawing materials were so constantly before him that his mother used to say, " When Johnny marries it will be to a paper wife." But he found the fight, handicapped as he was by poverty, a terribly uphill one, and discovered ere long, as many others have done, that it was easier to get praise than halfpence.

Eager for practice and instruction, and at the same time finding the need for money, the youth for a short time found employment with a portrait painter in Holborn. When at the age of fifteen or sixteen, he succeeded in placing himself under a teacher of the name of Joseph Charles Barron, who had a class for drawing twice a week at No. 12 Furnival's Inn Court. In return for tuition Varley was obliged to give some menial services, such as running errands and doing odd jobs generally, and this not only during the class hours, but at other times also. In addition he had to assist in teaching. He drew, however, with the other pupils, and was also instructed in etching. Among the youths he met here was Francia, one of Girtin's fellow-pupils, who was likewise an assistant, although in a higher position than Varley.

" Poor Varley," writes one who knew him well at this time—" Poor Varley began the world with tattered clothes and shoes tied with string to keep them on. Yet nothing," he adds, "could damp the ardour of his mind. His evenings were given either to drawing or to copying the works of the great masters, his favourites among the latter being Claude and Gaspar Poussin. Only when he could no longer hold up his head did he go to bed. Yet with the earliest dawn of day he was again astir, drawing indefatigably until it was time for him to go to business—whatever for the time being that might be. Then, with an old portfolio slung over his shoulder, he would start off full trot, and not stop till he arrived at his master's door."

Many of these details of Varley's early days we

owe to John Preston Neale, a brother-artist who, though about seven years his senior, did not take to art as a profession until a later period. According to Redgrave,[1] Neale began life as a clerk in the post-office; but he seems to have spent his leisure in the pursuit of tastes inherited from his father, who was a painter of insects. Early in March 1786 he went one Sunday morning to Hornsey Wood to sketch and collect insects. There he fell in with John Varley, who was likewise out sketching. They entered into conversation, and so commenced an acquaintance that lasted during their joint lives.

Becoming frequent companions on similar expeditions, Neale appears to have tried to inoculate Varley with his taste for entomology, but signally failed in the attempt. He persuaded him, however, to join him in a project for the production of a somewhat ambitious work on natural history. It was to be in royal quarto, and to be called the *Picturesque Cabinet of Nature;* consisting of landscapes, beasts, birds, insects, flowers, etc. Varley was to do all the landscape drawings; Neale was to etch them, as well as to make all the other drawings and colour the plates. The first number duly appeared (September 1796), and

---

[1] *Dictionary of Painters.*

consisted of three prints—of horses, cows, and an ass.

Neale gives the following graphic description of one of his sketching excursions with Varley in the same year. It was on a fine Sunday morning in spring, and John Varley and he sallied forth in search of the picturesque. "About seven A.M.," he writes, "we reached the private madhouse at Hoxton, and as the foliage was beautiful round its banks, we sat down to copy their beauties. We had been seated but a short period when we began to frighten each other by tales regarding the unhappy persons confined within this sad abode. Suddenly a terrible rush was heard among the trees and bushes. Having previously raised our fears to the highest pitch, we stayed not to inquire the cause ; but scrambling up, made a precipitate retreat to the middle of the field, where we stopped to watch the supposed maniacs that were making their escape. We then discovered our mistake, the noise being made by some men who were robbing the garden falling from a tree, and who were equally surprised with ourselves, supposing us there to watch their movements. Having been thus satisfied, we resumed our seats, finished our sketches, and proceeded to Tottenham, where we commenced sketching the church. . . . To give my friends some idea of our feelings at this time as young artists, it will be only necessary to state that we saw the people going to public worship; in the morning, in the afternoon, and in the evening they found us there. So exact were our notions that in colouring my sketch I copied the colours and even counted the bricks, minutely attending to every other particular. During the day we subsisted upon a crust of bread and water."

On another occasion they drew and coloured Stoke Newington Church.

Neale often visited Varley at his mother's house in the Old Street court, and he describes [1] a theatrical performance which they got up between them, hiring a room of a neighbour for the purpose, and losing money because the venture proved a failure. One of the pieces performed was "George Barnwell."

In a "Notice of the Life and Labours" of Cornelius Varley, drawn up during the latter's lifetime, and under his supervision, if not actually by his own hand, it is said that as a youth John Varley was so advanced in his studies that he "commenced teaching drawing." This may refer to the assistance he gave to his teacher Barron. The latter must have thought highly of his pupil's talent, for we find that he took him as far as Peterborough on a sketching tour. He made a drawing of the cathedral of that city, which

[1] Roget, *History of Water Colour Society.*

was greatly admired, and which subsequently was the means of winning for him his first fame as an artist.

Of evenings he was enabled to take advantage of the academy, or whatever it may be called, of Dr. Munro, who, to the profession of specialist in insanity, joined that of art patron and dealer. He had a house on the Adelphi Terrace, overlooking the river, and to it resorted many of the young artists of that time—probably, however, more with a view to profit than for study. For it was the habit of Munro to pay his students and retain their drawings and sketches. This, at all events, was his method with those who showed any marked ability, like Turner, Girtin, John Linnell, William Henry Hunt, and others, his scale of payment being from half-a-crown to three shillings an evening. Nor does Munro appear to have made a bad thing of it, since for some of the works thus acquired he seems to have obtained good prices.[1] But, taking his income from this source altogether, it must have been small in comparison with what he derived from his private asylums and from his position as one of the physicians who attended George III during his malady.

---

[1] Amongst John Linnell's correspondence is a letter from Munro, in which he refuses an offer made by Linnell for one of his drawings by Girtin, saying that he always looked upon it as an equivalent for a ten-pound note.

By these means Varley made rapid progress in the art he had adopted as his profession ; and in 1798, that is, when he was nineteen years of age, he exhibited his first picture, a " View of Peterborough Cathedral," at the Royal Academy.

CHAPTER II

THE GROWING MAN

FROM being an assistant to Barron, Varley soon developed into a teacher on his own account. He had already commenced to do a little in this line before sending his first drawing to the Academy; but the fame that he won by that exhibit speedily increased the number of his pupils, whilst it at the same time enabled him to increase his prices. In short, what with the sale of his drawings (for they were now in demand) and his tuition, he was ere long earning so handsome an income—for so young a man—that he was enabled to bring comfort back to his home, and to become the chief stay and support of his mother and his brothers and sisters. He at this time lived, according to the Academy catalogue, at No. 2 Harris Place, a sort of blind alley situated in Oxford Street, near the Pantheon. He subsequently moved from there to No. 5 Broad Street, Golden Square. This was about 1806, and his house here was shared for a time by William Mulready, who had just married his sister.

In the year 1799 he was again an exhibitor at the Royal Academy, his subject this year being "A View on the Thames." He continued to exhibit under the same auspices until 1804, when, in conjunction with others, including his brother Cornelius, who, like him, was devoted to landscape art, he helped to found the Water Colour Society.

In the "Notice" of Cornelius Varley above referred to, the latter claims to have originated the idea of founding the Water Colour Society. He says the notion occurred to him at St. Albans, and that "on his return to town his brother John called a meeting at the Stafford Coffee House, Oxford Street, to arrange the preliminaries and fix the time and place of meeting." After the foundation of the Society John Varley identified himself almost exclusively therewith.

Many of his subjects during these early years of endeavour were from the banks of the Thames, always a favourite resort of his, as it has been to many a landscape artist since. They bear undoubted evidence of having been painted on the spot, and are marked by great individuality and truth to nature—characteristics which are likewise stamped upon the drawings executed during three visits made at this period to North Wales, in whose wild mountain scenery he found the subjects best suited to his brush.

The first of these visits to the Principality took place in the summer of 1799; it was followed by others in 1800 and 1802. He made many studies during these tours, and these supplied him with the material for numberless pictures, with which, when the Water Colour Society was founded, he almost deluged its exhibitions, sending to the first no fewer than forty-two subjects (nearly all Welsh), and during the first eight years contributing in all 344 drawings. He also made a journey to the Northern counties for the purpose of study, but he did not there find so congenial a field for his art as in Wales, amongst the solitude of whose hills and vales he received impressions that powerfully influenced the whole course of his art.

On one of these visits to Wales the artist came near losing his life by being attacked by a bull. As he was seated sketching a bit of delightful scenery, altogether oblivious of any threatening danger, he was charged by an infuriated animal and tossed, together with his paraphernalia, several yards in the air, which, seeing that he weighed seventeen stone, was not a bad hoist for the bull.

This was only one of his "hairbreadth" escapes

from serious injury or death by the horns of bulls.
Once during the Old Street period he was attacked
and tossed by a bull in Old Broad Street Road and
much hurt. Somewhat later he was in still more
imminent peril of his life from a similar cause. He
was crossing one of the London bridges—Westminster, I believe—when an infuriated animal, which
was being driven to the slaughter-house by a butcher,
ran at him and threw him on to the parapet, over
which he was slipping when the man in charge of
the creature caught hold of the skirt of his coat, and
thus saved him from a watery grave.

When in after life Varley turned his attention to
astrology, he declared that, by reason of the conjunction of certain stars, he had from his infancy
been liable to casualties from the attacks of animals.
Whatever one may think of the prediction—if, being
after the event, it may be called one—certain it is
that he seemed destined by some untoward fate to be
subject to the onsets of infuriated animals. For at
another time, much later in life, he came very near
losing his life from a furious onslaught by hounds.
He was sketching at the Earl of Blessington's
country-seat when he got in the way of the hunt,
and the hounds set upon him with the utmost fury.
Every stitch of clothing was torn off his back, and
the maddened brutes would doubtless have done

him further hurt if the huntsmen had not just then ridden up and beaten them off. As it was, they found him without a rag upon his back. Either the Earl of Blessington or one of the gentlemen of the hunt lent him a cloak in his extremity, or he would have had to get back to his lodging as best he could without so much as Adam's primal covering to hide his nakedness.

A somewhat similar story is narrated of Cornelius Varley, although in his case the incident occurred in Ireland, whither, after a third visit to Wales (in 1805), he journeyed and made a number of sketches. Cornelius, who was of a genial and companionable disposition, like his brother, was greatly delighted with the Irish people, whom he found both warm-hearted and generous, though his enjoyment of the country was considerably dashed by an adventure he had one day while busy sketching. It was in the hunting season, and quite unknown to him a fox, slinking away from the hounds, took refuge under the camp-stool (or whatever it was) upon which he was seated, and over which he had thrown his greatcoat. In the course of a few minutes he became painfully aware of Reynard's malodorous presence, and rose, sniffing, to discover the cause; whereupon the fox quickly levanted. The artist, with a quiet chuckle at the animal's odd choice of a place of refuge, reseated himself and went on with his painting. But scarcely had he got to work again ere the hounds burst upon him, and finding the scent very warm, upset him and his traps in no time. Poor Cornelius found himself in a sad plight, and in his perplexity could think of nothing better to do than mount a convenient tree. The huntsmen, riding up a minute or two later, thought the hounds had "tree'd" the fox, and laughed uproariously when they found it was "only an artist." They joked him about his "brush," which he had dropped in his hurry to get up the tree, and treated him, as he thought, most unmercifully. They afterwards solaced him to some extent by inviting him to the hunt supper, but nothing would induce him to prolong his stay in the country, or to pay it a second visit.

But to return to the one who is more particularly the subject of this memoir. Much of John Varley's work in later years was executed in haste and without due care; but at this time, when he was at his best, he was undoubtedly a fine landscape painter, and many of his drawings will compare favourably with the best work of his contemporaries; albeit he may have been outdone by some of them, both in breadth of treatment and in grandeur of conception. His range was not a large one; but probably no one has done fuller justice to the sunlit slopes of Welsh mountains, or to the quiet vales and peaceful lakes of that delightful land. In this respect he opened out a new realm to the landscape painter, and showed to the art-loving world possibilities in water colours that had hardly been dreamed of before.

But in estimating his influence it must be borne in mind that he was the great art teacher of his time, and that his enthusiasm for painting in water colours amounted almost to a cult, and infected nearly all who came under his influence.[1] It was a saying of his that while painting in oil might be compared to philosophy, the practice of landscape in water colours must assimilate to wit ; and, considering the wonderful things that were done in his time, and the cleverer and more daring ones that have been effected since in that medium, the saying seems abundantly justified.

[1] As an instance of the way in which his enthusiasm infected others, the following anecdote may be given. One day when he called at the Earl of Blessington's to give a lesson to a member of the family, he noticed the lackey who opened the door for him slip something that looked suspiciously like a drawing-board behind a chair. "What is that you have put away?" cried Varley. The man blushed and said that he had been trying his hand at a drawing while seated in the hall. He had, he confessed, been so much interested by hearing Varley expatiate at his lordship's table on the glories and delight of water-colour painting, that he had expended a month's wages on drawing materials, and had gone to work in his spare time. "Let me see what you have done !" exclaimed Varley ; and some time later he was discovered by the Countess giving an impromptu lesson to the lackey, having completely forgotten that someone else was patiently waiting for his coming.

He put forth no exaggerated claims on behalf of his favourite art, and it may be somewhat in consequence of the modesty of their aim that the water-colourists of his school did so much. "While locality and texture is (*sic*) one of the great excellences of oil-painting, clear skies, distances, and water, in which there is a flatness and absence of *texturo*, are the beauties most sought after in the art of water colours." Such was his view of the general scope of water-colour painting, and within the limits thus indicated, few have done better than Varley at his best. Tranquil scenes of mingled hill and vale, quiet waters reposing in subdued sunlight or 'neath evening skies, or wide-rolling, verdant champaigns —these were the themes that Varley loved best to handle, and these he could touch and interfuse, as it were, with a brooding poetry. Stronger or more venturesome subjects he rarely attacked, perhaps because his sympathies did not run in that way, possibly because he doubted his powers of accomplishment, or the potentialities of his art. It remained for other men to give us pictures of storm and tempest, the turmoil of agitated waters, and the burning splendours of sunset and sunrise; he was content to wield a calmer brush, and to revel in quieter and more homely scenes.

CHAPTER III

As reference has been made to Cornelius Varley, and as he was a man of considerable mark in his day, it will not be out of place to give a few particulars about him here. As already said, he was some three years younger than John. Like his younger brother William and his sister Elizabeth, Cornelius appears to have been his elder brother's pupil; or, if they were not actually his pupils, they owed much in respect to their art development and training to his example and instruction.

Cornelius was born at the house in Hackney on the 21st November 1781. The earliest impression that he was wont to refer to, was an accident that might have cost him his life. When four years old he fell head foremost from a first-floor window. Fortunately he descended upon a flower-bed the earth of which had been newly turned, and to its softness he attributed his safety from harm, as he could well remember his father taking him to see the impression his head had made in the ground.

His father died when he was ten years of age, and he continued his studies at home until he was twelve, occupying his leisure time by going out with his elder brother to sketch. At that age he went to live with his uncle Samuel Varley, the watchmaker and jeweller, who was doing a thriving business. Like his brother, Samuel Varley seems to have been a man of considerable attainments in science, and something of a genius to boot, and under him his nephew Cornelius obtained an insight into many cognate arts, besides being initiated into the mysteries of watchmaking. He first learned the art of working jewels, and on one occasion when soldering a diamond in the steel mount with a blowpipe, he saw it catch fire and burn with a blue flame. This phenomenon, which is now well known, was at that time new, and was not fully confirmed until some years after Cornelius Varley's observation. Diamonds are now frequently burned in oxygen, and the exhibition of the experiment constitutes one of the most instructive chemical experiments of the present day.

Samuel Varley possessed air-pumps, electrical machines, telescopes, microscopes, and generally an extensive collection of chemical apparatus. These had a greater attraction for young Cornelius than watchmaking. His uncle had made some small microscopic lenses, and Cornelius, who had mastered the art of making jewelled holes for watches, turned his attention to making lenses as his uncle had done, although with only partial success until he devised the method of polishing them by making the tool of a composition of bees'-wax hardened by oxide of iron; and for the smallest lenses a composition of still tougher material made with shellac hardened with polishing powder. This mixture is universally employed by opticians at the present day. By his fourteenth birthday Cornelius had made his own microscope, the lenses and the whole of the mechanism being of his own manufacture.

In 1794 his uncle began a series of chemical experiments, and as he required a large room for the purpose, he took the celebrated Hatton House, which then had the reputation of being haunted. Here they carried on their experiments and founded a Chemical and Philosophical Society, of which the famous Josiah Wedgwood and other eminent men became members. These meetings and lectures and those of the old Philosophical Society were the forerunners of the formation of the Royal Institution in the year 1800.

On one occasion, when his uncle was delivering one of his chemical lectures at Hatton House, Cornelius was busy in an adjoining room preparing the oxygen for one of his experiments. During the operation the retort exploded, smothering him in black oxide of manganese, and making him as black as a sweep. However, he carried in the gas, for which his uncle and the audience were waiting, without stopping to consider his sooty condition. When he appeared in the lecture-room there was a hearty laugh at his expense. The incident gained for him the sobriquet of " Varley's Devil," a name by which he was known to some of the older members of the Royal Institution for many years ; indeed until he was long past middle age he was often so called.

Many of the earliest experiments with compressed carbonic acid gas for freezing mercury were made at Hatton House, where was devised and constructed the first apparatus for charging water with the gas under pressure, thus originating the manufacture of soda-water. In the sketch of Cornelius Varley above referred to, the writer says that, among other things that were done at Hatton House, "they made and erected a large electrifying machine with a conductor twelve feet long, and produced with it many very interesting and useful experiments which advanced materially the knowledge of electricity and electrical science."

Cornelius still continued to fill up his spare moments by making lenses, and he succeeded in producing one of $\frac{1}{100}$ of an inch focus, which was exhibited at various scientific meetings, and was decided by all present to be the most perfect that had then been produced. Thus encouraged, Cornelius made several such lenses, for which purpose he constructed special lathes for working and polishing them. These special tools, as well as his observations upon the microscope, and a number of investigations relative to animal and vegetable life which he made therewith, formed the subject of several communications addressed by him to the Society of Arts, for which he received on various occasions the Society's awards of silver and gold medals.

Earl Stanhope, who was one of the patrons of the Hatton House lectures, about this time asked Samuel Varley to join him with a view to helping him to perfect his discoveries in stereotyping. He consented, and his time being thus fully occupied, the Hatton House lectures came to an end, and soon after the Royal Institution started into life.

Cornelius now turned again to art, joining his brother once more on expeditions to sketch from nature.   John had now acquired fame as an artist, and it was his success, both as a teacher and in the sale of his works, that probably induced Cornelius to relinquish those scientific pursuits for which he seemed so strikingly fitted, in order to resume his studies in art.   Like John, he came for a time under the influence and patronage of Dr. Munro, and that gentleman introduced the two brothers to the Earl of Essex and to "the Prince Lascelles" (as he was then popularly called), afterwards better known as Lord Harewood.   He turned his attention also to teaching, and both he and his brother obtained many pupils through the recommendation of the Earl of Essex, who not only gave them great encouragement, but aided them with his advice as a friend, suggesting the amount they should charge for giving lessons, and so forth.

In June 1801 Cornelius was invited to Gillingham Hall, Norfolk, where he gave lessons in drawing from nature to Mrs. Bacon-Schutz and her daughter, as well as to some of their relatives.   This change from the work of the laboratory, notwithstanding the great fascination the latter had for him in appeasing his thirst for investigation and research, was a very happy one, and he felt the hardest day's work he then did in drawing from nature was "a glorious holiday."   He was of a most genial and contented disposition, and became almost at once a universal favourite in all societies with which he mixed. The period of these excursions and visits to various country seats was one of thorough, earnest, and truly healthy enjoyment. The pure air, the sense of liberty in roaming about and exploring the works of creation, and the certainty of receiving a hearty reception whenever he returned indoors, there to be surrounded by the most cultivated and amiable kindness that removed all care and brightened hope, "left with him" (to use his own words) "an impression upon his mind that nothing could efface."

From Norfolk he went into Suffolk, making numerous sketches. He remained there till midwinter, sketching out of doors all day long, often amid frost and snow.

During this tour of mingled sketching and lesson-giving the artist became painfully aware of his deficiencies in respect to perspective, and he returned to London in the early days of 1802 in order to lessen his ignorance. In the course of a few months he made himself thoroughly acquainted with the laws of perspective, and from that time was able to give his pupils instruction in what was then a greatly neglected department of study, and one which artists had for the most part entirely overlooked.

In the month of June he travelled into North Wales, where he was joined by his brother John and Mr. Thomas Webster, the architect of the theatre of the Royal Institution. While there he made drawings of Snowdon, the Pass of Llanberis, Dolgelly, Beddgelert, Carnarvon Castle, Harlech, Cader Idris, etc., after which he returned to Chester, going thence to Chepstow. In 1803 he made another tour in Wales, being accompanied on this occasion by John Cristall and William Havel.

In 1804 occurred the visit to St. Albans, where, as he says, he conceived the idea of the Water Colour Society. He went there to make some drawings to illustrate a work by G. Lewis. At the first exhibition of the newly-formed Society he exhibited what he calls "coloured sketches and views" of St. Albans and of the Market Place, Ross, Hereford, and other places. Truly at this time water-colour drawings were little more than coloured sketches, and the colours indeed were very watery, not to say washy; but the art gradually improved under the influence of the men who constituted the early members of the Water Colour Society, together with colourists like Holmes, Richter, and others.

CHAPTER IV

WILLIAM MULREADY AND SONS

IN the year 1803, at the age of twenty-four, John
Varley married Esther Gisborne, a sister of John
Gisborne, the friend of Shelley, with whom, as well
as with Godwin, the poet's future father-in-law, and
his set, he appears to have been well acquainted.
Another sister of Gisborne's became the wife of
Copley Fielding, the artist; while a third was married
to Muzio Clementi, the composer and pianist, and
improver of the pianoforte (afterwards associated
with a leading firm in the manufacture of pianofortes),
whose talents won for him a resting-place in the
cloisters of Westminster Abbey.[1]

---

[1] At the early age of twelve Clementi wrote a successful Mass for four
voices, and had made such progress in the pianoforte that Mr. Beckford
brought him (from Rome) to this country to complete his studies. He
was then engaged as director of the orchestra of the opera in London;
and his fame having rapidly increased, he went in 1780 to Paris, and in
1781 to Vienna, where he played with Mozart before the Emperor. In 1810
he settled down in England, where he died in 1832. His most important
compositions were his sixty sonatas, and the collection of studies known as

During these years John Varley had not confined his attention solely to art, but, like his brother Cornelius, had given much time and attention to the study of science. But the "science" to which he more particularly devoted himself was that of astrology, in which he became one of the greatest adepts of his day. Among fashionable people he was better known as a "ruler of the planets" than as an artist, and many persons, while ostensibly calling upon him to see his works, were in reality more attracted by his fame as an astrologer. Nor, seeing that he was never loth to be drawn out upon his favourite subject, did they often go away without being given an opportunity of testing his powers in that respect. Had he been living at the present time instead of fifty years ago, he would undoubtedly have run the risk of being sent to jail as a rogue and vagabond—if, that is, as is said, he was always ready to take his fee for casting a horoscope. There is considerable doubt, however, as to whether he ever did take money for such services. It was always a hobby of his to draw the nativity of persons he met, and to amuse them by his predictions. He would hardly have done this if he had

the *Gradus ad Parnassum*. He represented perhaps the highest point of technique of his day, and his influence upon modern execution led to his being characterized as "the father of pianoforte playing."

looked upon his astrology as a money-making affair.

Nor would there have been anything very blameworthy if he had by this means added a little to his income, which in the early days of his marriage was probably small enough, though what with his art and his teaching (of which he had very soon as much as he could manage), it must ere long have been very considerable for one of his years and position. But whatever his income, such was his kindness of heart (which made it impossible for him to refuse to help a friend in need) and such his unbusiness-like habits, that even in these early days he was never long out of money difficulties. One of the first effects of his disadvantages in this respect was that he was thrown very much into the hands of the dealers, and from this circumstance doubtless arose much of the weak and common-place work with which his name is unfortunately associated.

Among the number of his pupils were William Mulready, R.A., who, as already stated, married one of his sisters; William Henry Hunt, the fruit and flower painter, and delineator of scenes in humble life; John Linnell, the famous landscape artist; Francis Oliver Finch, who became a member of the Royal Society of Painters in Water Colours;

William Turner of Oxford, a landscapist of great talent; Samuel Palmer (who was his pupil for a short time); Ziegler, a German Swiss; to say nothing of a host of others who had not the good fortune to attain to equal fame with some of these.

Hunt and Linnell were under Varley at the same time. Linnell records[1] how he was once making sketches of pictures in Christie's sale-room in King Street, St. James's, when he was accosted by William Fleetwood Varley, who admired his drawing, and advised him to go and see his brother John. The young artist did so, with the result that his father agreed to place him under Varley's tuition for a year, giving him a premium of £100. Linnell says that he first saw Varley in a little house in Harris Place, Oxford Street; from which he removed to No. 5 Broad Street, Golden Square. He had a cottage also at Twickenham, where his pupils lived some part, if not the whole of the time, for the convenience of sketching from nature. Linnell and Hunt spent most of their time in this way, now on the river, now in the lanes and fields, drawing, as Varley told them, "everything in nature, and in every mood." He was an enthusiastic admirer of nature himself, and he generally

---

[1] *Life of John Linnell.*

succeeded in inoculating most of his pupils with his enthusiasm.

Linnell, in some autobiographical notes which he left behind him, has much to say about his master, and especially about this early period of their acquaintance. Judged by this record, as well as by the reminiscences of all who knew him, John Varley must have been possessed of very exceptional qualities even among men of genius. Not only was he a man of genial character and amiable disposition, but one of large and liberal views, and full of striking and original conversation. His house was the resort of wits and men of talent and education in every branch of art and the professions, and he attracted and delighted all alike by the kindliness of his heart and the extent and variety of his knowledge. Something of the quality of the man may be gathered from the fact that he was as full of play as of work, that he indulged in both with equal vigour in due season, and that he never thought of himself when he could help a friend. Such was the amiability of his disposition in this latter respect that he would often put teaching and commissions in the way of his friends that he might have had himself.

He was especially fond of boxing, and he used to vary the tedium of painting and teaching by an occasional bout with the gloves. His studio was often the scene of a lusty set-to of this description, especially if his brother-in-law, Mulready, happened to drop in, he also being a great adept in the art of self-defence. Mulready, being younger and not so stout as the somewhat heavy and elephantine Varley, generally had the best of it at these diversions; but, discomfited or not, Varley enjoyed the fun, and after a good laugh and a rest for wind, he would come up again, smiling and undaunted.

Everybody in their circle, indeed, appears to have caught their enthusiasm for boxing (which was one of the fashionable crazes of the time), not excluding even the diminutive Linnell, who refers in his Autobiography to these pugilistic encounters with a zest which half a century of toil and religious meditation had failed to weaken. He speaks of others who took part with them in these exercitations, and records, not without a touch of pride, that upon the walls of his lumber-room still hang the veritable gloves that had drawn George Dawe's "claret."

Mulready was a pupil of the Jew pugilist, Mendoza, and he is said to have been the best scholar that worthy ever turned out. He was a man of splendid physique and enormous strength. No end of stories are told of his prowess in this direction. He is said to have made the acquaintance of Mr. Sheepshanks, the art patron, by defending him when attacked by a number of London roughs. Nor did his bout of fisticuffs prove a bad piece of business, considering the number of commissions it was subsequently the means of bringing him.

Once a hackney coachman demanded of him an exorbitant fare, and when Mulready would not pay it, he became exceedingly abusive and offered to strike him. The artist thereupon threw off his coat, and the two stood up at the corner of Great Portland Street and Oxford Street and fought for an hour, Mulready at length doubling up his man and coming off victorious. The fight was witnessed by a couple of thousand people.

Mulready and Sir John Swinburne, uncle of the poet, were walking one evening near to the gates of Holland Park, when a man came out of the public-house opposite and rudely attempted to push between them. They, naturally enough, resented the insult, whereupon the fellow struck Mulready. The artist, carefully judging his distance, struck the man a blow between the eyes, felling him to the ground like an ox. Sir John, afterwards narrating the circumstance, said, " It was a most fearful blow. I heard it echo among the trees overhead."

Mulready had four sons, all big strong men, taking in this respect after both the Varleys and the Mulreadys. Their names were Paul, William, Michael, and John. They were all nearly as expert boxers as their father, who appears to have taught them impartially both the arts in which he was *facile princeps*. But while one of them at least was his equal as a boxer, none of them came in any way near him in regard to the art of painting. They all became artists, and made their living in that way, but chiefly by portrait painting and teaching. All of them, however, had the one fault: they were too academic, with the result that they were stilted in composition and style, and so never came to the front.

A singular story is told of Paul Mulready, the eldest of the Academician's four sons, touching his fame as a pugilist. He was one day going out of his house in Bayswater when he was met at the gate by a rough-looking fellow and incontinently knocked down. Picking himself up as quickly as he could, Paul naturally asked the man to what he was indebted for the blow. "Why, you see," said he, " I'm the Somers Town champion, and I 'eard as 'ow you was a fust-rate boxer, Mr. Mulready, and so I thought I'd come and 'ave a turn with you." Paul replied that, seeing that he had made so free with his fist, he would indulge him, and asked him where he proposed the contest should take place. The answer of the Somers Town champion was to the effect that he had already been to the landlord of the Rose and Crown opposite, and that that gentleman had consented to let them have a room and see fair play. The proposal was agreed to; and the story goes that the worthies fought all night, and in the end finished with a drawn battle, so well were they matched. But Mulready gave his antagonist such a dressing that he never fought again, while he himself was confined to his bed for several days after the event.

Albert Varley, John Varley's eldest son, was Paul Mulready's executor and the guardian of his son. When Paul was on his death-bed Varley went to see him. He found his old friend greatly affected at the prospect of his approaching dissolution. "Good-bye, Albert," he sobbed at length, "I shall never see you again. You have always been a good friend to me, and I don't know anyone that I have thought so much of. But, my dear boy," he added, "you ought to have fought the barber." Varley thought his friend was surely wandering, and replied that he did not understand him. "Don't you remember," Paul asked, "how when we were boys together, you and I and Michael once threw stones at a barber's apprentice, and he challenged you to fight, and you would not; the result being that Michael, who had to take your place, got a tremendous hiding? He will never forgive you to his dying day. He has told me so often—he told me so again the last time I saw him. I have always taken your part; but I think you ought to have fought the barber."

When it was thus recalled to his mind, Varley recollected the circumstance, and could only be surprised at the way in which the ruling passion still showed itself strong in death.

Another anecdote of the family's boxing propensities is equally well worth recording. The sons never got on well with their father, any more than he did with his wife. Referring to these causes of difference one day when with Albert Varley, Paul said, " Well, I can forgive my father for all that he has done wrong towards us except one thing, and that I will never forgive him for as long as I live." "And what is that?" asked Varley. Paul then explained to him that one of the first principles of the pugilistic art was in fighting not to keep the fist tightly clenched all the time. By doing so the muscles and ligaments of the forearm become strained and too soon tired, whereby the boxer is unable to continue to deliver his blows with all the force that he otherwise would. The proper way, he explained, was to keep the hand flexed but not tightly closed until actually about to deliver the blow, when it should be strongly clenched. "Now," said Paul, with vehement indignation, "my father knew that secret for years, and never told me! It was a mean thing to do, and I will never forgive him—never!"

After Paul's death, amongst other documents was found a letter from his mother. It was a recent one, and was to the following effect: "My dear son, bear in mind that you are now nearly sixty years of age, and remember what your uncle, John Varley, predicted about this year. Do not box or play at cricket, for you may receive an injury to your knee or leg which may prove fatal."

The prediction referred to was contained in the horoscope cast by John Varley at Paul's birth sixty years before, and was remembered by his mother, who knew how apt her brother's prophecies were to turn out true.

It happened, however, that one day in the summer of this year Paul went to Kennington Oval to see a cricket match, when a ball, driven from a long distance, struck him on the knee. White-swelling was produced; he was ill for a long time, and finally the leg had to be amputated. It was taken off by Dr. Holmes Coote, and the patient died under the operation.

John Varley was quite as fond of boxing as Mulready, and had he been less ponderous in size, he might have shown equal prowess as either he or his sons. As the case stood, however, it was used more as a means of exercise and relaxation than for attack or defence. The gloves always hung up in his studio, and nothing pleased him more than to put them on and confront his doughty brother-in-law. Occasionally, in order to vary the fun and excitement, they would put off the gloves and toss Mrs. Varley from one to the other across the table, she screaming, while the rafters resounded with their laughter.

They must have been gay, laughter-loving times, those of our grandfathers at the other end of the century, and not a little uproarious to boot.

All Mulready's sons lived to an advanced age except Paul, who, as we have seen, died at the age of sixty. Michael, the second, was over eighty when he died. All four of them were born before Mulready was twenty-one years of age, he having married Varley's sister when he was seventeen. When he was little more than twenty-one he separated from his wife, and they never lived together again. Incompatibility of temper was generally supposed to be the cause of their separation; but though this may have been the main difficulty between them, the real reason for their final quarrel and parting was the fact that Mrs. Mulready, who, like her brothers, was a talented artist and frequently exhibited, used to go into her husband's studio when he was out and work upon his pictures. Mulready was a very slow worker, sometimes devoting a year to a single picture, and the wife doubtless thought she could expedite matters, and bring a little more grist to the mill, by lending an occasional helping-hand. But the R.A. who managed to put up with a good deal, felt obliged to draw the line at having his pictures touched upon by his wife.[1]

[1] According to Mulready's own statement to a friend (from whom I had my information), Mrs. Mulready, when out of humour, used to go into his studio and paint out the eyes of his figures.

CHAPTER V

BUT we are getting along a little too fast. Mention has been made of Varley's eldest son Albert, whose second name was Fleetwood. Besides him there were four other sons: Henry, Frank (who was subject to fits and died young), Charles Smith, and Haydon, the latter named after Varley's friend Benjamin W. Haydon, the painter. Then there were three daughters: Emma, Susan, and Esther. A characteristic story is related respecting the naming of the artist's fourth son, Charles Smith. When the time arrived for him to be christened Mrs. Varley was too ill to leave her bed. She kept reminding her husband, therefore, not to forget to have the child christened in time, but he as constantly put the matter off. Finally, when it was not possible to delay a day longer, he sent the servant with the child to the church. She herself acted as godmother, but as no one had been provided to stand as godfather, she asked a stranger who happened to be present if he would act in that capacity, and so relieve her from a difficulty. He consented, but when the girl asked him his name, he appeared reluctant to take any responsibility in the matter, and replied, "Oh, Charles Smith." So the boy was called by that name.

Although so good-natured and even tender-hearted, John Varley was not the one to spoil his children or his pupils by over-indulgence. With both he was a severe disciplinarian. Finch tells how, if he heard a noise in the room above his studio, where the youths were at work, he would suddenly take a cane out of a drawer, rush into their midst, administer castigation freely all round, and as suddenly disappear. It was the day of such exercises ; the tenets of Solomon were observed in all their glory, and John Varley followed them like the rest. Even the dog would come in for a share of the blows if he did not behave himself. Finch records that on one occasion the dog set up a barking when a visitor called. Out came the cudgel, and the dog was speedily reduced to silence, when the rod was put away with the remark, "I hate affectation."

Varley's son Albert frequently bore testimony to his father's peculiarities in this respect. "If we got up to any mischief or skylarking, and made a noise, the next thing was a vision of his yellow dressing-gown and brass-edged ruler. He did not stop to ask who was the ringleader or the greatest culprit, but treated all alike with the greatest impartiality, not even sparing a visitor, if we should happen to have one."

He was a great advocate of cold-water bathing, and in order that there might be no lack of this, he had a tank made at the end of his garden, into which, seizing each of his sons by a leg and an arm, he plunged them, neck and crop, three or four times every morning, and then sent them off to dry and dress. If they howled too much over these rough ablutions, he gave them an extra dip.

Varley was a tremendous worker. Always up by daybreak, he set to work at once, and did not intermit his industry until day was done. He used to say that for forty years he had worked on an average fourteen hours a day. He did not even stop work for his meals ; but a corner of the cloth was turned up, and there while he ate he worked at his drawings. His attention was given so thoroughly to what he was doing that he took little notice of the food that was put before him. Once, it is said, two horribly bad eggs were given to him by mistake, but so intent was he upon the drawing before him that, though the others were offended by the smell of the eggs, he went on eating them as though they were most deliciously fresh.

George Goodban, the artist, who married Varley's daughter Susan, called one day, and finding him busy in his studio, said, "Well, have you anything ready for the Water Colour Society?" Varley replied, "God bless my soul, no! When is the day for sending in?" Goodban told him that it was in five or six weeks. Varley replied, "I must begin on something at once." When the day for sending in arrived he had forty-two drawings ready. The prices ranged from 5 guineas to 250. All, or nearly all, were sold; the Prince Consort being the purchaser of the highest priced one.

As reference has been made to his food, it will be convenient to say here that the artist was as abstemious in regard to drinking as to eating. He cared little for liquors of any kind, and seldom indulged in anything stronger than a little table-beer. Even that was ordinarily too strong for him, and was usually diluted with water to obviate its intoxicating effects. His tea too had to be of the weakest description. His money, therefore, of which he made so much and kept so little, did not go in self-indulgence or in feasting.

In short, he was an enthusiast, and as such gave

but little attention to anything save his art, or the "science" of astrology to which he was so devoted. Every morning, as soon as he rose, and before he did anything else, he used to work out transits and positions for the day, or what astrologists designate "secondary directions and transits." Thus he would work up his own horoscope for the day. As an example of what this means I may give the following interesting incident, which shows something of the character of the man, as well as the nature of his astrological studies.

One morning while living at Bayswater Hill he sent his son Albert out immediately after breakfast with his watch to get the exact time at a watchmaker's close by. When he returned with the time Varley went over his calculations again very carefully. Still not being satisfied, he sent the boy out again to see if the time was exact. When he returned the second time, saying the watch was right, Varley said, "I can't make it out; there is something very serious going to happen to me to-day so many minutes before twelve o'clock, but whether the danger is to me personally or to my property I cannot tell."

He went on to explain that the planet which was thus menacing him was Uranus, which, having been but recently discovered, was something of a puzzle to astrologists, because its astrological powers were not yet well understood. He had an engagement that morning, but he was so anxious about the threatened danger that he would not go out. His reading of the aspect of the heavens was to the effect that the peril would be sudden and serious. Thinking therefore that he might be run over or get a tile on his head, or suffer some such accident, he thought it would be prudent to risk nothing, and so remained at home.

As the hour of twelve approached he became greatly agitated, and walked up and down his studio unable to settle to anything. A few minutes before the hour he said to his son, " I am feeling all right ; I do not think anything is going to happen to me personally ; it must be my property that is threatened."

Just then there was a cry of fire outside. He ran out to see what was the matter, and found that it was his own house that was in flames. " He was so delighted," said his son Albert, describing the occurrence—" he was so delighted at having discovered what the astrological effect of Uranus was, that he sat down while his house was burning, knowing though he did that he was not insured for a penny, to write an account of his discovery. He had timed the catastrophe to within a few minutes. He knew the square or opposition of Uranus would have a bad effect, but in what way he could not tell. Although he lost everything in the fire, he regarded that as a small matter compared with his discovery of the new planet's potentiality."

However much deception there may be in astrology (of which I leave others to judge), there can be no doubt of Varley's *bona fides* in the matter. He thoroughly believed in the "science," and if there was deceit, he was the subject of it as much as anybody who went to him for his forecasts. Many are the stories told of the wonderful predictions he made, and how astonishingly they were verified. On one occasion he drew the horoscope of the children of an artist friend, James Ward, and made some revelations so astonishingly true that the father had the documents destroyed, as indicating beyond doubt some commerce or collusion with the father of lies.

No one could come in contact with Varley without speedily being made aware of his leaning to astrology. It was "a mania with him, and his common theme at table," says one who knew him well.[1] "He was no sooner introduced to a friend than he would ask him the date of his birth, and having obtained that knowledge, he would quickly make out the stranger's horoscope." Gilchrist in

----

[1] My informant was Mr. William Vokins, the picture-dealer.

his *Life of William Blake* gives some anecdotes of his success in this direction, and others are recorded in the *Life of John Linnell.* Some of them are astonishing enough, as, for instance, the statement that he foretold the death of William Collins, R.A., to the very day years before the event took place; also the declaration made by Scriven, the engraver, to the effect that certain facts of a personal nature, which could be known only to himself, were nevertheless confided to his ear by Varley to the smallest particular.

Nor were these by any means the most remarkable of his astral revelations or vaticinations. On one occasion he drew the horoscope of a young lady who was then about sixteen years of age. He told her that she would marry in the course of a few years, and that there would be one child issue of the marriage. But, having gone thus far, he suddenly stopped and exclaimed, "Hallo! what is this? a second marriage!" Then he added after a pause, "There is something wrong here." The young lady asked him to explain, but he declined to do so. What he saw was that the second marriage was to take place before the death of the first husband. Hence his hesitancy and doubt. But the sequel of the lady's history proved the truth of his reading of the horoscope.

She was married to a clergyman, who was vicar of a parish somewhere in the east end of London. A few years after their union, however, he left her, disappearing so completely that she neither saw nor heard of him for a long time. Then, after a lapse of some ten or twelve years, she received a letter from him. He was in Australia, and the letter stated that he had made his fortune at the gold-diggings. A draft for a large amount was enclosed, and with it the wife was instructed to furnish a house and expect his coming to join her in a short time. Nothing more, however, was heard from him, and though the wife caused inquiries to be made respecting him, she could learn nothing for several years, when she heard that he was dead. Some time after this she married again, her second marriage proving a very happy one. Subsequently, however, it turned out that the one-time clergyman was not dead, but was still living in some part of Australia. His strange conduct appears to have been due to insanity. Thus was Varley's prediction strangely proved to be true.

Here is another of his astrological vaticinations. One morning when he and two friends—probably artists—were in the country they set out for a walk. Before they started he said — having doubtless worked his transits for the day—"We shall witness some horrible accident before we get back." In the course of their walk they came to a river over which a railway bridge was being built. Workmen were busy driving piles for the foundations, and as they stood and watched the operations, a man, who was leaning over one of the piles to do something, was crushed to death by the falling hammer, the trigger of which had been accidentally pulled. When they got back to their inn one of the men said, "Well, you said we should see a horrible accident, and we have seen one—a horrible one indeed!"

On another occasion he sent his son Albert to deliver a drawing to a gentleman who had given a commission for it. When he got to the house he found that it was not in the portfolio. In consequence of being insecurely tied, it had doubtless slipped out at the end while the boy was going carelessly along. When he reached home he was afraid to tell his father of his mishap, anticipating a jacketing for his negligence. Varley, however, looked at him steadily and said, " Did you deliver that picture?" The boy, trembling, answered that he had not, explaining the accident. "I did not think you could have delivered it," replied Varley very quietly, to the boy's great relief. "I foresaw from the aspect of the stars that I should have an accident with a drawing to-day."

Mr. William Vokins informs me that Varley was at his house when his daughter was born. As was his custom, he at once, on hearing of the event, took out a piece of paper and cast the infant's horoscope. When it was done he turned to Mr. Vokins and said, "Be very careful of the child when she is four years of age. At that time she will be in danger of a severe accident from fire." The parents did not take much notice of the prediction, and had indeed almost forgotten it, when, at the age named, the little girl was so severely scalded that her life was for some time despaired of. She lost both hearing and sight, and was thus afflicted for two or three years. Finally, she regained her sight, and to some extent, though not fully, her hearing.

Varley made a similar prediction in regard to Wakley, the well-known truculent and radical member of Parliament of those days, editor of the *Lancet* and coroner for Marylebone.

Another story connected with his astrological leanings is as follows. Once his son Albert, who was then married, went to dine with a famous Scotch physician. In the course of the evening the doctor said, "Why, Albert, you have a very bad cold. I must give you a prescription that will cure it." When Albert Varley was about to leave, his friend wrote out the prescription and told him to get it made up at the nearest chemist's. It was late, and when he got to the first chemist's shop the man was just about to close the door. He consented, however, to make up the prescription, but in his hurry he forgot to put a label on the phial. When he got home Varley took the whole of the contents of the bottle, and at once fell insensible on his bed. In course of time he woke up, but was unable to move. He sent for his friend the doctor, and told him that he had taken the dose that he had prescribed, but that it had disagreed with him. "Did you take the whole of it?" asked the doctor. "Yes." "I don't wonder it disagreed with you; the wonder is you are alive. The phial contained forty doses." Albert Varley had a prolonged illness, and at times it was not thought he would recover.

John Varley was at this time living at Kentish Town, which was then really a country suburb. One day he walked down to see how his son was progressing. He had found by consulting his astrological books that it was a critical day, and he was extremely anxious, and remained with the patient until the hour of danger was past.

He appears, however, not always to have been equally happy in his forecasts—if, that is, we are to believe the report of the late Sir Richard Burton. The famous Oriental scholar and traveller was well acquainted with Varley in his younger days, and he told the artist's grandson and namesake, whom he met in Egypt, that he had learned how to draw horoscopes from his grandfather. In the Life of Burton recently published by his widow, he is quoted as saying, "Mr. Varley was a great student of occult science, and perhaps his favourite was astrology." He adds, "Mr. Varley drew out my horoscope and prognosticated that I was to become a great astrologer; but the prophecy came to nothing, for although I had read Cornelius .Agrippa and others of the same school at Oxford, I found Zadkiel quite sufficient for me."

Burton was not the only famous man who was indebted to Varley for aid and guidance in occult studies. Amongst others who went to him for instruction in the quasi-science of astrology and allied subjects was Bulwer-Lytton, whose predilection for studies of this kind is manifest in his novels *Zanoni* and *A Strange Story*. He and Varley worked at astrology together, and in the occult machinery of the works named Bulwer is said to have been much indebted to suggestions given to him by the artist.

One of the three works to which Varley appended his name is a *Treatise on Zodiacal*

Physiognomy.[1]   It is a curious work—what there is of it, for it was never completed, only one of the four projected parts appearing; but the theories enunciated in it are clear enough.   He holds (with Ptolemy and other ancient writers) that persons born under certain signs have certain well-defined lineaments of face, and that for this reason not only their characters and dispositions, but to some extent their fortunes also, can be read in their countenances. In his preface he says : " The apparent power of the various signs of the zodiac in securing a diversity in the features and complexions of the human race " is "as well established among inquiring people as the operation of the moon on the tides, and may be properly termed a branch of natural philosophy." But, though he goes on to affirm that "it is a subject capable of much more ample and ready proof than the astronomical fact relating to the tides," he unfortunately fails to make it clear to the unenlight- ened reader.   Indeed, he does not seem to try; he gives us such statements as that, though "Lord Byron was born under Scorpio," he "received enough of the Taurus principle to prevent his nose from being

---

[1] Its full title is "A Treatise on Zodiacal Physiognomy, illustrated with Engravings of Heads and Features, accompanied by Tables of the Rising of the Twelve Signs of the Zodiac ; and containing also New and Astrological Explanations of some of the Remarkable Persons of Ancient Mythological History."

aquiline, and to give to his character a degree of perverseness or eccentricity ; " but he does not show us by what subtle chains or gradations of influence the zodiacal sign of the Bull militates against the enjoyment of a straight nose.

Among the "heads and features" illustrating the text (which are from the drawings of his friend Linnell) there appears Blake's portrait of the "Ghost of a Flea," of which he says that "it agrees in countenance with a certain class of persons under Gemini, which sign is the significator of the Flea, whose brown colour is appropriate to the colour of the eyes of some full-toned Gemini persons." In this sentence we have a slight indication of the way in which we come by the colour of our eyes, but it still leaves us in the dark as to the exact astral influences that make or mar a perfect nose.

In this amusing little work the author hazards several vaticinations, of one of which Lord Rosebery would do well to take note. So far as one can gather from the somewhat vague phraseology, it predicts that Ireland will not make much headway in the line of her present political aspirations until the year 2001. At that time, however, she will experience "the regard of a great monarch, and probably of a great continental nation, and of the people signified by Virgo," whoever they may be.

"Englishmen will then make choice of many Irish ladies for their wives, and the country may, under the auspices of this star (Regulus), become eminent for the education of females!"—which of course signifies the very best sort of Home Rule.

In his day Varley's fame as an astrologer made him almost better known among a certain class of people than his celebrity as an artist. One who knew him well says he has seen him the centre of a group, consisting of ladies of aristocratic position, well-known authoresses, and others, who hung upon his words while he told their fortunes, in which he became so absorbed as to forget the lessons he should at the time have been giving. It was a common thing for him to question people whom he met casually as to the date of their birth. Having obtained the desired information, he would proceed to draw their horoscopes and tell them their future. In this way he would frequently be able to tell a person that he was in error as to the time of his birth, explaining that as Jupiter (or it might be some other planet) was at the time in such and such a conjunction, his countenance must necessarily have been quite different from what it was if he had been born under the aspect of the heavens prevailing at the reputed time of his birth. On the same principle he was able, it is said, from a person's physiognomy to name the star, or conjunction of stars, under whose influence he was born.

In addition to his *Zodiacal Physiognomy*, Varley was the author of two other works, both of them on the art upon which rests his more permanent title to fame. One is entitled *Observations on Colouring and Sketching from Nature*, and the other *A Practical Treatise on Perspective*. The former was to have been completed in twelve numbers, but four only were issued. They were published by the author himself, who, on the cover of the work, gives his address as 44 Conduit Street. Each part contains a couple of landscapes in monochrome, and these serve as texts for the author's remarks. Although without any approach to style, often even without grammar, they are ably put together from the artist's point of view. What he has to say is clearly and concisely stated, and his views on light and shade, colouring, and composition are so well stated that the merest novice cannot rise from the reading of them without bringing away very definite notions as to the scope and methods of the art of which Varley was a master; while to the young beginner in water-colour painting they would be invaluable. The wonder is that this treatise, together with that on Perspective, has not been republished with annotations bringing it up to date.

CHAPTER VI

THE most interesting period of Varley's life—to the literary world at least—is probably that which brought him in contact with the mystical painter and poet, William Blake. This may, roughly speaking, be said to comprise the period from 1819 to 1826. He was introduced to Blake by his former pupil, John Linnell, who was, at the period named, married, and steadily making his way to the success and fame which he subsequently—though not till comparatively late in life—achieved.

Linnell's first meeting with the dreamer took place in 1818, the two being brought together by the younger Mr. Cumberland of Bristol. As Linnell and Varley were at that time residing near to each other, the one in Cirencester Place and the other in Great Titchfield Street, and frequently met, it is more than likely that the introduction occurred at Varley's house, where they subsequently often met in the evening.　Sometimes Linnell would be present, an attentive observer and listener, taking everything in, but saying little.　On one occasion he made a characteristic sketch of the two as they were arguing together.[1]　It shows Varley alert, eager, inquisitive, Blake calm, thoughtful, contemplative.　What a contrast they present!　It would be hard to find two men more opposite in their general qualities, and yet they were perfectly at one in regard to their belief in the possibility of the ghosts or spirits of men dead making themselves visible to the living.

Thus when Blake had got his seeing cap on, Varley, sitting by, would say—I quote from Gilchrist : "' Draw me Moses,' or David ; or would call for a likeness of Julius Cæsar, or Cassibellaunus, or Edward the Third, or some other great historical personage.　Blake would answer, ' There he is!' and paper and pencil being at hand, he would begin drawing with the utmost alacrity and composure, looking up from time to time as though he had a real sitter before him ; ingenuous Varley meanwhile straining wistful eyes into vacancy and seeing nothing, though he tried hard, and at first expected his faith and patience to be rewarded by a genuine apparition. . . .

---

[1] Reproduced in the *Life of Linnell.*

"Sometimes Blake had to wait for the Vision's appearance; sometimes it would come at call. At others, in the midst of his portrait, he would suddenly leave off, and, in his ordinary quiet tones, and with the same matter-of-fact air another might say, 'It rains,' would remark, 'I can't go on,—it is gone! I must wait till it returns'; or, 'It has moved. The mouth is gone'; or, 'He frowns; he is displeased with my portrait of him,' which seemed as if the vision were looking over the artist's shoulder as well as sitting *vis-à-vis* for his likeness. The devil himself would politely sit in a chair for Blake, and innocently disappear."

The portraits were often criticised, but Varley never doubted their genuineness. He believed implicitly Blake's statements in respect to them, and indeed appears to have regarded them as perfectly authentic.

In the way described, Blake executed for Varley, always in his presence, some fifty or more pencil drawings of these historical or mythical personages. They were generally of small size, although two, now in the possession of his grandson and namesake, are larger. They are carefully drawn, and rather pleasing in expression, albeit somewhat feminine. One represents Jonathan, the friend of David, and the other Harold the Second after the Battle of Hastings.

Most of the Heads were subsequently purchased by John Linnell, and are still in the possession of the family. The majority bear the date August 1820, but a few were executed nearly a year earlier. The name and date are in the handwriting of Varley, who is very explicit in his description. Thus one is endorsed " Richard Cœur de Lion, drawn from his spectre. W. Blake *fecit*, Oct. 14, 1819, at quarter past twelve, midnight." There is a second inscribed " Richard Cœur-de-Lion," and different from the first. Another is described as " The Man who built the Pyramids, Oct. 18, 1819, fifteen degrees of 2, Cancer ascending." In a third we have " Wat Tyler, by Blake, from his spectre, as in the act of striking the tax-gatherer, drawn Oct. 30, 1819, 1 h. P.M."

But the most curious of all the Visionary Heads, or Heads from the Spectre, and the one that has perhaps excited the greatest curiosity, and called forth the most remark, is the " Ghost of a Flea." Of it Varley gave an engraved outline and a description in his *Treatise on Zodiacal Physiognomy*. The latter is sufficiently singular, and at the same time characteristic of the author, to be worth quoting. It is as follows : " This spirit visited his (Blake's) imagination in such a figure as he never anticipated in an insect. As I was anxious to make the most correct investigation in my power of the truth of these visions, on hearing of this spiritual apparition of a Flea, I asked him if he could draw for me the resemblance of what he saw. He instantly said, ' I see him now before me.' I therefore gave him paper and a pencil, with which he drew the portrait of which a facsimile is given in this number. I felt convinced, by his mode of proceeding, that he had a real image before him ; for he left off, and began on another part of the paper to make a separate drawing of the mouth of the Flea, which the spirit having opened, he was prevented from proceeding with the first sketch till he had closed it. During the time occupied in completing the drawing the Flea told him that all fleas were inhabited by the souls of such men as were by nature bloodthirsty to excess, and were therefore providentially confined to the size and form of insects ; otherwise, were he himself, for instance, the size of a horse, he would depopulate a great portion of the country."

The *Treatise on Zodiacal Physiognomy* contains also an engraved outline of another of the Spectre Heads—that of the Constellation Cancer. Coloured copies of three of the Visionary Heads — those, namely, of William Wallace, Edward I., and the Ghost of a Flea—were made for Varley by Linnell.

It is worthy of note before closing this chapter

that Linnell, who, knowing both men intimately, was well qualified to judge, considered Varley to be of a more credulous turn of mind than Blake. This, indeed, appears to have been one of the weak points in his character. A phrenologist of that time—a man of some eminence in the world of science and letters, and well known to Varley—attributed to him excessive credulity. "He believed nearly all he heard, and all he read," was his judgment upon him. It appears to have been borne out by his phrenology, a science which scientific men had not yet learned to taboo because unfashionable.

Varley tried hard to convince Blake of the truth of astrology, but could never make much headway in that direction. It involved a theory too material-istic for the transcendental spirituality of the mystic.

Curiously enough, too, neither Blake nor Linnell—both strongly religious men, though differing on points of doctrine—could make any impression upon Varley's scepticism in regard to current religious dogmas. Though credulous to the last degree, the spiritual was a realm to which he seems to have had an utterly blind eye. According to Mr. Atkinson—above quoted—he knew no distinctive God or creed. "He belonged to no sect, took no private road, but looked through Nature up to Nature's God."

Could there have been a finer exemplification of

the truth of Gall's doctrine of the plurality of faculties than these three men presented—Varley, Blake, and Linnell? Here was a trio devoted heart and soul to art, full of genius, full of enthusiasm, and yet in all other respects how different! In Blake we see the calm, confident transcendentalist, a man who with the inward eye looked sheer into the spiritual world, the full and complete circle, so to speak, of which this nether and outer world is but a broken and imperfect segment; neglecting this world, and in turn neglected of it; a mere child, in fact, so far as earthly things go, but spiritually a man of such stature as the world seldom sees. Varley was the converse of all this. Worldly to the last degree, all his schemes, ideas, and feelings were stamped as of the earth earthy. Though extremely credulous, and ready to believe on the least, or even on no evidence, yet when it came to the supernal wonders, the divine attributes, manifested on every hand, there was no sentient tablet to receive impressions; his mind was there a blank.

In Linnell we see again a different type. In him we have a more fully rounded and filled out man, and yet he too had his frailties. With genius perhaps greater than either, greater even than Blake in respect to art, more normal and manageable; with the same fine spiritual turn, though wedded to less heterodox views, he was nevertheless far from being, like Blake, disqualified by his unworldly powers for the business of the world. Indeed, he possessed a superabundance of those prudential faculties of the mind that specially qualify a man for worldly success. In this respect he could set an example to the physical and material Varley. In truth, it might have been better for his fame if he had been less gifted in this respect, as it made enemies for him among those of his profession who were less successful than himself; it appears to have caused him enemies too among dealers, who found in him a match for themselves in all that concerns business matters. The latter are pardonable, but it is hard to find words of condemnation strong enough for brother painters who, in order to justify their injustice to him, invented falsehoods to prove him to be unutterably selfish and mean.

That he was " canny " no one can deny ; but that he was so despicable as to make his aged father pay five shillings a week for his board while living under his roof one cannot believe without doing violence to one's feelings. Yet it is stated on the authority of someone who pretends to have witnessed the scene, that on one occasion he was present at the artist's tea-table when a white-haired old man whom he did not know entered the room and took his place with the rest. A mug of tea and a plate of bread and butter were placed before him ; but before he touched either he took five shillings from his pocket and pushed them with a trembling hand towards Mr. Linnell, saying, " Here is my week's money, John. Let me have a receipt for it." A receipt was at once pencilled on a bit of paper and handed to him. The old man scanned it carefully, then, as he folded it and put it in his pocket, he turned to the stranger and said, "That, sir, is the way father and son do business." The fact that the story has been given to me in three different versions, each fathered on a different person, is perhaps proof sufficient of its utter lack of foundation in truth.

That John Linnell was very keen after the shekels, very shrewd in driving a bargain, and equally · cautious not to be done in any way, is beyond doubt. There are many anecdotes — genuine ones — in attestation of the fact. Perhaps the following is as good and characteristic a specimen as could be found, and it has the merit of being perfectly authentic, as I have it on the authority of Mr. J. L. Budden (of Messrs. Budden, Fisher, and Company, of Lime Street), who writes :—

" John Linnell was sometimes at my office to see my partner, Mr. J. H. Spencer (since dead), who had lived in Oporto, and was a first-rate judge of port wine. They on one occasion went to the vaults of the London Dock and selected for him a pipe of genuine fine port wine. After they had done this, Linnell turned to the cooper and borrowed his scribe (with which the casks are marked), and stooping down with the lamp, and using the tool on the head of the cask, he returned it to the man, saying, 'There! you won't imitate that.' The cooper, after inspecting the cask head for a short time, exclaimed, 'Why, sir, it's your own profile!' And so it was. A few days after he went to the dock in a cart, and after getting the pipe out of the bonded customs vaults, duty paid, he rode home with it among the straw in the cart, 'with his martial cloak around him.'" Mr. Budden adds: "If this cask head were still in existence it would be a curiosity."

As Varley's residence in Great Titchfield Street has been referred to, it may be as well to say that I understand it was here that he suffered great loss from being burnt out. On two other occasions he was subjected to a similar disaster: one has been already referred to in connection with his astrological leanings; the other fire, his grandson, John Varley, informs me, took place in Conduit Street, where he had a gallery as well as a studio.

CHAPTER VII

THAT Varley was a most original and eccentric character there can be no question. All who knew him, or were in any way brought in contact with him, agree on this point. Linnell, who, as we have seen, lived in his house for a year, and from 1805, when they first became acquainted, until 1842, when Varley died, knew him intimately, has but two criticisms to make against him. One is, that he was lacking in the qualities that constitute a shrewd, successful business man ; the other, that he was not of a religious turn, or, in other words, that he was. not much given to church-going or to dogmatic religion. In spite of these defects, however—and they were the negative of the qualities upon which his critic set the highest value, and were those which characterized him the most—Linnell's admiration for Varley was very high. He was accustomed to say, and indeed he wrote in his Autobiography, that Varley was possessed of many noble qualities, and that, while he was not a religious man, he was not a hypocrite. It is curious to note too this further judgment, namely, that he might not have been a better man, even if so good, had he made a profession of religion. One can well believe that. Popular religion—the all-absorbing effort and desire to save the soul, or the skin—has a tendency to make men selfish; and this Varley could not be. He was indeed the very antithesis of selfishness. Mr. William Vokins, one of the few persons still living who knew Varley well, bears emphatic testimony to his unselfish disposition. " His kindly, unsuspicious nature," he writes, " was constantly bringing him into difficulties. He could not say ' No ' when his purse or name was of any use, and it was no uncommon thing for him to lose a lesson (the fee for which was one or two guineas) in order that he might aid some case of distress. But more than this—he would often give to others who were in need what he actually wanted for himself, and so put himself in the most unheard-of difficulties. Nor was it always the deserving he thus assisted; often enough the very opposite was the case; for, as Linnell says, he profited scarcely at all by experience, and put implicit confidence in the most treacherous and crafty people. Indeed, though a man in stature and years, he seems to have retained to the last the simple and unsuspecting heart of a child."

He was indeed of such an easy-going, sympathetic disposition, that he absolutely could not refuse to help others when in difficulties. He was constantly being asked to put his name to bills, and he as constantly consented. Invariably, of course, he had to pay or go to the sponging-house as the result. Things at last arrived at such a pass that he did not feel that all was right unless he was arrested for debt at least once or twice a month. With the utmost regularity the tipstaff would make his appearance and say, " Mr. Varley, I am afraid I must trouble you to come along with me." Varley took the visit as a matter of course, replying, " Just wait a minute until I put together a few materials, and I shall be at your service."

The materials were a portfolio with two or three boards, colours, brushes, etc. With these, as soon as he arrived at the place of detention, he would rapidly execute a couple of drawings, and when they were finished he would get the bailiff to take one to his friend Mr. Vokins, and the other to another dealer, and with the proceeds pay off his debt. No wonder much of the work of his later years was of a somewhat slipshod character.

In one year he had upwards of thirty writs served upon him, and most, if not all, of them for the convenience of other people! Again and again had he to suffer arrest and go to the sponging-house, with the result that he was obliged to pay double or treble the amount of his debt before he got free. Yet nothing broke the spirit of the man. Always cheerful, hearty, and brimming over with kindness, he would even protract his stay in the house of detention in order to cheer and hearten the downcast and despairing men whom he found there who were not able to bear up under their load of trouble and worry as he did.

He even found a beneficent providence in his tribulations. "All these troubles are necessary to me," he once said to his friend Linnell. "If it were not for my troubles I should burst with joy!" Nor were his debts his only troubles ; for, besides a son grievously afflicted (with epilepsy or some kindred disorder), he had a helpmate, who, though she was not wasteful and extravagant, yet lacked the ability to make up for his unbusinesslike disposition. Gilchrist says she "dissipated as fast as he could earn" ; but that gentleman was too apt to take any one's tittle-tattle as evidence of truth, much to the detriment of his otherwise very interesting work.[1]

[1] The *Life of William Blake.*

Here is an instance in point. Speaking of Varley's astrological leanings, he says he was "not learned or deeply grounded, or even very original in his astrology, which he had picked up at second-hand." This is the reverse of fact. There may not be much to be said in favour of a "science" the principles of which appear to be based on a wild and untenable theory; yet what there is of it, that Varley seems to have known well and thoroughly. In fact he was such an enthusiast on the subject that he would often devote hours to it that would have been better perhaps and more profitably spent in painting or teaching. There is probably a considerable amount of truth in Linnell's criticism upon him when he says that, though he was always calculating nativities, he could never calculate probabilities. Or, did he place too much reliance on the "promise" of the stars, and find them fail him at the last moment? This would be quite like him, with his immense faith, his easy good-nature, and his unquenchable friendliness.

"He was a most sincere and kind-hearted friend," says Mr. Vokins—too often to his own hurt and undoing, as would appear. · "It was extraordinary," says Linnell, "how easily Varley acquired a large and valuable professional connection among the nobility and others, and how ready he was to recommend to their notice and employment his brother-artists. I believe Mulready was greatly indebted in that way to Varley." He adds that all his acquaintance benefited by his generous activity to serve them, and no one more, perhaps, than himself.

As to his character in other respects, Gilchrist pictures him not untruthfully, although with a touch of caricature, as was his wont, and apparently his delight. Contrasting Blake, Linnell, and Varley as they appeared to an eye-witness (possibly Samuel Palmer) at Linnell's place at Hampstead "in animated converse," he presents us with the following picture : "Blake, with his quiet manner, his fine head—broad above, small below; Varley's the reverse. Varley, stout and heavy, yet active, and in exuberant spirits—ingenious, diffuse, poetical, eager, talking as fast as possible. Linnell, original, brilliant, with strongly-marked character, and filial manner towards Blake, assuming nothing of the patron, forbearing to contradict his stories of his visions, etc., but trying to make reason out of them. Varley found them explicable astrologically—'Sagittarius crossing Taurus,' and the like ; while Blake, on his part, believed in his friend's astrology to a certain extent. *He* thought you could oppose and conquer the stars."

To this picture Gilchrist adds that " Varley was

a terrible assertor, bearing down all before him by mere force of loquacity. . . . But there was stuff in him. His conversation was powerful, and by it he exerted a strong influence on ingenuous minds." Then we have this further touch, again with a slight leaning towards caricature: "Varley was a genial, kind-hearted man; a disposition the grand dimensions of his person — which, when in a stooping posture, suggested to beholders the rear-view of an elephant—well accorded with." Truly he was of a broad, solid build, heavy in mould, and not much like an artist to casual lookers; indeed, more like a farmer in appearance; generally somewhat untidy in his dress, wearing at all times and in all seasons a tail-coat with great salt-box pockets—a not uncommon habit in those days.

These pockets were apt to be stuffed full with all kinds of indiscriminate odds and ends calculated to be of use some time or other. But, whatever else happened to be there, one article was never wanting, namely, a plenteous supply of pills. These were not of his own invention and manufacture, as it has been the habit of some to represent, but were made on the prescription of a well-known doctor of that day, and, like many others, were held to be good for most of the ills that flesh is heir to. At least, Varley had faith in them; and used to carry them about with him, and prescribe and give them freely to all and sundry who appeared in any way to be ailing. One day he was accosted by a poor fellow whom he met by the wayside, and who asked him for alms. "I have not, unfortunately, a single copper left," replied the famous painter with unfeigned regret, "but" (taking a box of pills from his pocket) "here is a box of pills which I will give you; they are excellent things—good for almost every complaint." The beggar took the pills with a rueful countenance, doubting probably whether they would quite meet his particular case, but unable to refuse them from so genial a giver.

These pills, still known as "Varley's Pills," are sold and ·taken—doubtless with as much benefit as the generality of such medicaments—to this day.

This habit of carrying about pills was so peculiar that nearly every one who came in contact with Varley was made aware of it—even to the conductors of the omnibuses running from Bayswater to the City. There was a standing condition of hostility between them and him on account of his enormous size, which caused him to take up the room of two ordinary persons. For this reason the conductors were wont to pretend not to see him when he hailed them; at other times they would shake their heads when he made signs for them to stop, and he was obliged to offer double fare in order to get them to take him up. But even that bribe would not always tempt them to do so ; accordingly he was in the habit of conciliating their hostile mood by an occasional gift of a box of pills.

In respect to size and girth, he presented a striking contrast to his second wife (a sister of Joseph Lowry, the inventor of a machine for line engraving, which entirely revolutionized that art), to whom he was married in his later years. She was as thin and lath-like as he was broad and stout, and many were the jokes passed at their expense ; which, however, never disturbed Varley, whatever may have been their effect upon his better-half. She appears to have been a most excellent woman, affectionate and devoted to the last degree, and so far as her husband put it in her power to do so, made his later years happy and comfortable. All who knew Mrs. Varley spoke in the highest terms of her many good qualities, and it is said that when she became a widow Bury the architect sought her in marriage.

Notwithstanding Varley's almost inexhaustible good-nature and kindliness of disposition, there was one source of annoyance which tried his patience exceedingly, and which he often said had caused him more chagrin than almost all his other troubles put together. This was the disgraceful conduct of his son-in-law, George Pyne, who had married his daughter Esther, a woman as high-minded and as refined in manners as he was the reverse. There appear to have been no depths of infamy to which this creature could not sink. Though wedded to a woman as comely as she was accomplished, and as fondly devoted to him as wife could be until his habits made him an object loathsome to every decent-minded person, he used to leave her for the worst sinks of vice ; whence he had repeatedly to be redeemed, his clothes and everything he had having been pawned or sold for the wherewithal to carry on his debauch.

Although a clever artist, he was too erratic as a worker and too unstable as a man to be able to carry on an independent home, and so he was allowed to share the house of his too-indulgent father-in-law, with the result that Varley was frequently obliged to support both him and his wife, when he was too idle or in too vicious a mood to work. Nor was this the worst of the matter ; for when the wretch had not the means, the fruit of his own industry, to indulge his appetite, he would steal from his wife's father, sneaking into his room at night and taking the money from his pocket, and robbing him in any other way that chance afforded. Yet this was a man of so much natural talent that he could have earned any amount by his brush had he been so minded, while he was the author of one of the best works on perspective that has ever been written. Fortunately, the new divorce law came into operation in time enough to enable his wife to get rid of him, and to become the companion of a man who was better worthy of her and made her in every way a happy and contented woman. Esther Varley's petition is said to have been the second under the new law.

This Pyne, the ne'er-do-well husband of Varley's daughter, should not be confused and confounded with another Pyne of Varley's acquaintance, namely, J. Pyne, better known as "Walnuts-and-Wine Pyne" —a very different man, and of a very different character, from the one described above. J. Pyne was one of the original eight or nine artists who founded the Old Water Colour Society, and a man, one would think, after Varley's own heart; at any rate he would appear to have been very much after his pattern—in one respect at least.

At one time he came into a legacy of £300, and, thinking it too small a matter to invest, he put it into a bag and hung it up by the fireside. Whenever anything was wanted, it was, "Well, take a guinea out of the bag." But to his astonishment, in the course of a few days, when he was in need of a little money himself, and went to the bag, he found it empty.

A similar story is told of Wills the dramatist. Whenever he drew money for a picture or for one of his plays it was put on a shelf over the door, and whoever wanted money simply reached up and took what he had a mind to. As Wills had many pensioners, as well as many parasites, and all were in the habit of helping themselves, it may be imagined that the hoard never lasted long.

CHAPTER VIII

ALTHOUGH troubles thickened with his increasing years, Varley to the end preserved the same hopeful and amiable disposition; he never lost his faith in men, nor any of his willingness to help them, even to the extent of greatly inconveniencing himself and his family; while his energy for work, whereby he still hoped to overcome all his difficulties, remained unimpaired to the last. He was, indeed, one in ten thousand—a man such as, in the main, the world needs more of.

Enthusiasms like his, whether for art, science, or literature, are as the salt of the earth, and preserve it from the canker of either selfhood or worldliness. His imprudence and lack of business judgment occasioned him many miseries, although he regarded them rather as wholesome checks to his otherwise too great happiness; but the world derived nothing except gain from the enthusiasm he had for his art.

That he would have done better for the
world in this respect but for his improvidence is
undoubted.   For, falling into the hands of the
dealers, and not being able to go to that Nature
which had been his early inspiration, his later works
were more or less of the nature of compositions
merely.   He had probably his early sketches in
Wales and elsewhere to go by, but his resort was
chiefly to the stores of memory, whence he derived
an almost endless series of pictures of mountain
and lake scenery.   Thus, though possessing many
of his distinctive qualities, they became mannered
and conventional, and not in any way comparable to
the work of his early and middle period, in which
we find such a breadth of effect, combined with
such simplicity of treatment, that they, together with
the works of Bonnington and one or two others of
their school, so aroused attention in France and
stimulated imitation, that they laid the foundation of
modern landscape art in that country.

Varley's best works are pre-eminently distinguished by these two great qualities of breadth and
simplicity.   His tints are refreshingly light, with a
full and free pencil ; and his colour is fresh and
pure.   Body colour is rarely, if ever, used in his
best works, and seldom indeed do we find a man
better versed in the rules of composition, which he

applied with the aptitude of true genius. He had, in truth, an inborn instinct for composition, which he had further strengthened by making himself master of its principles. Few can read his treatise on the subject without being convinced of the fulness of his knowledge of composition, even if they had not obtained such conviction from his drawings.

He was weakest perhaps in his foliage, which he treated rather as a mass than in individual detail. In the delineation of mountain scenery he has had few equals. Ruskin in his *Modern Painters* calls attention to this quality in Varley, and says that Turner and he were the only men he knew who could draw mountains.

As already said, he usually confined himself to the more everyday aspects of nature, to common sunlight and the fulness of summer foliage, rarely venturing upon autumnal tones or sunsets or their effects. We occasionally meet with the effects of light and shade in mountain valleys or amid cleft rocks, with still reflecting water, that exhibit here also the seeing eye and the master hand.

He did not feel strong in regard to figures, and used frequently to get other artists to put them in for him, as in his " Burial of Saul," one of the few pictures in oil that he executed, the figures of which were painted by his friend Linnell.

Varley almost invariably used a paper prepared by himself, and subsequently called by his name. It consisted of ordinary whitey-brown or thin yellow paper laid down on good Whatman paper. This gave him the rich warm tone to work on that he so much affected. If he wanted to get a brilliant point of light, he would just moisten the surface with a handkerchief and rub it clean away. Many of his finest sunset effects are obtained in this way.

His son Albert was at one time in the habit of using the same kind of paper, and on the occasion of a visit paid to Paris in 1826 he brought home with him a wire-marked cartridge paper made in Holland, which his father greatly admired and used much of. This was an imitation of what was known as his paper, and was called by his name. A manufactory in Holland was making this paper within a few years past, and possibly may be still.

His last great trouble, which probably shortened his days, was, like so many previous ones, the result of his utter inexperience in business matters. He had, in common with his brother Cornelius, inherited from his father a gift for mechanics and invention, and generally had some mechanical contrivance on hand. In his later years his ideas ran chiefly on the improvement of carriages. His place at Bayswater Hill was strewn all over with wheels, in the construction of which he had hit upon some secret, or conceived he had, by which the draught of vehicles would be greatly facilitated. But though he spent both time and money on his invention, nothing came of it—nothing, at least, except further trouble.

He took out a patent for his invention—a cab with eight wheels, which by some sort of compensatory action were supposed to render the vehicle both safer and swifter. Such, at least, is the account generally given of the thing. But it did not come up to expectation. Indeed, the first trial with the cab proved so disastrous that the man who had advanced the money in order that the invention might be tested and the patent secured was nearly shaken to pieces in it. He was a nervous little man, with a somewhat slipshod hold on life, and when he had once landed out of the vehicle in safety he exclaimed, "Never no more, Mr. Varley—never no more! Ten minutes in the thing has all but shaken the life out of me; ten more would quite finish me. Never no more, thank you, John." The old gentleman was so emphatic that it became a byword among Varley's friends when speaking of his invention: " Never no more, thank you,

John." Varley never heard the words which brought the scene to his mind but he laughed till his sides ached.

And yet it was no laughing matter. The scheme which was started to work the invention turned out so disastrous that it proved to be the last straw that broke the camel's, one might almost say the elephant's, back. In order that Varley might participate in the expected profits of the undertaking, a friend, as already said, agreed to advance £1000. Unfortunately the advance was made in acceptances instead of in money. Varley discounted the bills and acquired a share; but his friend failed to honour the bills when they matured, and the scheme ending in failure, the discounted bills were thrown back upon Varley, who was unable to meet them. Great embarrassments followed; writs were issued upon his furniture and effects, and also upon his person.

In his extremity Varley reaped the reward of previous kindnesses shown to a poor fellow who was obliged to act as jackal to a notorious bill-discounting lawyer of Golden Square, whose clerk he was. One who knew the man describes him as a sort of Newman Noggs, and his master as another Jonas Chuzzlewit, whom he thinks Dickens must have known, if he was not, indeed, the original of that famous creation. The man's name was Righey, and he and two others of his cloth, named respectively Theobalds and Reynolds, were never long without having their clutches upon poor Varley. Reynolds, be it said to his honour, only took 5 per cent for his discounting transactions, but he had in addition to be sweetened with presents of drawings—from Varley, that is. Whether it was his custom in like manner to require "inducements" in kind from his other clients is not recorded, but after a visit to one of his lawyer friends Varley one day staggered into the shop of a friendly dealer weighed down with a load of pickles, which the worthy had compelled him to buy. Said Varley, as he disgorged the bottles, one after another, from his pockets, "There's a lot of them; but they will come in useful; and I had to do something to put him in a good humour."

The clerk in question was deputed to serve Varley with a writ, but instead of doing so he took the artist to his own humble lodging, over a tripe-and-trotter shop in Gray's Inn Lane. Having thus placed him in safety, he took a note for him to his friend Vokins, who at once hastened to his assistance.

Mr. Vokins found him in great discomfort, but as usual still cheerfully at work. This had always been his panacea for every evil, and his never-ending solace in trouble; and now, in his sixty-sixth year, he was as sanguine as ever and talked as confidently as ever of the industry and perseverance that would soon overcome all difficulties. But, as the sequel showed, his hopper of work had been filled and there was little more for him to do.

On the following day he was got away from the tripe-shop by stealth, and conveyed to Mr. Vokins's private residence at 67 Margaret Street, Cavendish Square. There the artist remained six weeks in hiding, painting away as indefatigably and as hopefully as ever, for the most part happy and cheerful, though worried in mind and not well in health.

One of his last acts before being carried off by the lawyer's clerk was to go to the gardens of the Royal Pharmaceutical Society, Chelsea, to make a sketch of a famous cedar there. In order to do this he sat upon the damp grass. As the result he caught a severe cold, which flew to his kidneys, resulting in severe inflammation. He took but little notice of it at first, thinking that the confinement and want of exercise had resulted in a slight attack of indigestion. One day, feeling very low, he thought he would like some stout. This was got for him, and he drank it; but so unused was he to such potations that the effect of it was to increase the inflammation to such an extent that his death speedily ensued.

During his stay with Mr. Vokins he was visited by many distinguished persons. Hearing that Mr. Varley was staying with him, they would beg to be introduced, " not more," says Mr. Vokins, " for his artistic celebrity than for his astrological knowledge, and for the interest there was in the man himself, for his was a most genial spirit."

He was visited too, as a matter of course, by his friends, his son Albert being frequently with him. To the latter he said one day, as he sat by his bedside, " I shall not get better, my boy. All the aspects are too strong against me for me to recover." He had, as usual, been consulting his astrological books, which were at the time lying on the bed beside him.

Thus did this extraordinary man pass away, mourned and lamented by all who knew him— grieved over even by men like the poor lawyer's clerk, who had only come in contact with him casually and as an embarrassed debtor ; but even to such as he Varley could not help showing his true nature and disposition, kindly and good-natured to the core.

There appears to have been something as extraordinary about his sudden demise as about his life. The doctor who had attended him could not make it out, and in order to resolve his doubts, he asked permission to make a post-mortem examination. He was a surgeon at one of the hospitals, and after making the autopsy, he brought some of the students to see the body. " I want," he said, " these gentlemen who are studying medicine to see the body of a man of his age who has the organs of a child." The heart, lungs, liver, all the organs, in fact, except the kidneys,[1] were in a perfectly healthy condition, and "as though," to use the surgeon's expression, "he had never used them." The doctor added that this perfectly normal condition of the organs was one of the most marvellous things he had witnessed in the whole course of his experience.

Mr. Vokins, in a few notes he gave me about Varley for my *Life of John Linnell*, says he doubts if the former ever had an enemy. But he appears to have had one at least—perhaps the only one. Mr. Vokins was a personal and deeply-interested witness of a scene in which this individual mani-fested his hostility.

At a meeting of the Phrenological Society, held in Exeter Hall shortly after Varley's death, a paper was read upon his phrenological peculiarities, illus-trated by a cast of his head.[2] The writer of the paper held that the conformation of the skull was singularly

---

[1] One of the kidneys weighed 6 oz., the other 16 oz.
[2] This cast is now in the possession of his grandson and namesake.

confirmatory of the science of phrenology. A discussion followed, in which much was said pro and con., although nothing derogatory to the high character of the deceased. But finally a man rose from the body of the hall who took quite an opposite view to all that had been advanced. He said that he had known Varley personally, and that so far from his developments being in favour of phrenology, they were quite the reverse ; for, instead of being the generous, liberal-minded man he had been described to be, he held him to be little better than an impostor.

Considerable excitement was caused by this address, which was delivered by John Lewis senior, the engraver, who, it afterwards turned out, had been under no small obligation to the man whose memory he traduced. Such is gratitude !

However, there was one present who was both able and ready to speak in favour of the deceased artist. This was Mr. Vokins, who happened to be in the gallery. He was observed by someone who knew him and his connection with Varley, and Dr. Elliotson, who occupied the chair, was asked to call upon him to speak. Invoked thus by name, he rose and spoke at some length in vindication of his friend's character for unselfishness and liberality. He was himself indebted to him for numberless acts of kindness, and he knew many others who were equally his

debtors.   Referring to these, he concluded by saying that if Varley did err—and undoubtedly he did
—it was in consequence of the inherent and unquenchable generosity of his spirit, and from the fact
of his being unable to say " No."

Mr. Vokins spoke warmly and with enthusiasm,
and carried the meeting with him almost to a man.

Mr. Vokins concludes his story by saying that on
the following morning a gentleman holding a high
position in the Civil Service left his card at his business place, and said how much he should like to see
him.   On their subsequently meeting, the gentleman
thanked him very warmly for his vindication of
Varley, and remained on the most friendly terms with
him to the day of his death.

The *Edinburgh Phrenological Journal* for 1843
contains a report of the proceedings at the meeting
here referred to.   It was Mr. Atkinson, F.S.A.,
who read the paper " On the late John Varley, the
eminent painter."   He described him as having been
a man of wonderful genius and intellect, original in
all his conceptions, grand in all his designs, and
an ardent admirer of Nature and Nature's works.
" He loved the sublime and beautiful, the cloud-capt
mountains, the lovely valley, the placid lake, the
umbrageous wood impervious to the sun.   These
were his delights to view, and these he was enabled to

transfer to canvas. In landscape painting he stands pre-eminent; none have excelled him; few can equal him. He was the founder of this species of art in water colours. In manners he was lively, affable, benevolent, and communicative; his charity was as large as his expansive heart. He knew no definite God or creed. He bowed to no sect, he took no private road, but looked up through Nature to Nature's God. As our memory has its dark side, so has human nature its frailties. Varley's may have been quite amiable—it was credulity. He believed nearly all he heard—all he read. He was an astronomer and was deeply impressed with the occult science of astrology. He imagined the starry hosts to possess an influence over the actions and feelings of men, and that there are more things in heaven and earth than are dreamed of in our philosophy. Varley was wholly devoted to worldly pursuits, and was consequently always in difficulty. A cast of his head was exhibited. The coronal region was large, the social faculties fully developed, and the intellectual of a high degree. Ideality, his predominant sentiment, was strikingly large, also benevolence and constructiveness."

CHAPTER IX

VARLEY, the incomparable, was survived by both his brothers. William, who, like his brothers, turned his attention to teaching, had gone to Cornwall about 1810, where he taught with much success, as afterwards at Bath and Oxford. At the latter place, in consequence of the thoughtless frolic of a party of students, he was nearly burned to death. As it was, his nerves suffered a shock from which they never recovered. In his later years he was sheltered in the house of his son-in-law. He died at Ramsgate in February 1856, at the age of seventy-one.

His other brother, Cornelius, survived him thirty-one years, dying on the 2nd of October 1873, at the advanced age of ninety-two years. Of this worthy's youthful achievements in science something has already been said. It may be added that in 1809 (when he was twenty-eight years of age) he invented what he called the Graphic Telescope and Portable Table, by which, in an artist's hands, portraits from life and views from nature can be taken with greater facility and accuracy, of any size, and in correct perspective. With this instrument, which he turned to much use, Cornelius Varley made many sketches of country scenery, drawings of machinery, as well as pencil drawings from life. He subsequently improved the telescope, and had it patented in 1811. Hereupon a difficulty arose; the opticians of that day were not sufficiently advanced in the science of their trade to manufacture these instruments. This made it necessary for the inventor to turn manufacturer, which he did with some regret, his desire being to devote all his time to art and scientific research.

The Colosseum, the institution in Regent's Park so well known in former years, built for the reception of the panorama of London, had its origin in the invention of the Graphic Telescope. Mr. T. Horner, the originator of the panorama, after having satisfied himself of its capabilities, erected an observatory in the dome of St. Paul's, fitted up one of these instruments, and so traced his gigantic picture.

From this time forth Cornelius Varley's time was divided between mechanical pursuits and the arts. He made many improvements in the microscope, devising among other things the lever microscope for watching the movements of animalculæ. For this invention he received the gold Isis medal of the Society of Arts, of which he had become a member in 1814. He was a frequent visitor at Kensington Palace, the Duke of Sussex, who was then president of the Society, giving soirees there, at which Varley exhibited his microscopes and other apparatus. It pleased the little man greatly when His Royal Highness on one occasion said, "I need not remind you, Mr. Varley, that there is always a knife and fork laid for you here." There was not in Cornelius the sturdy independence and the indifference to rank and fashion that there was in his brother John, and it must at the same time be said, there was none of that incapacity to look after his own affairs that the elder displayed.

At the formation of the Royal Institution Cornelius Varley became a member, and at the first Friday evening meeting he exhibited the very first diamond lens that had then been made, whereby a great increase of aperture as compared with glass was obtained, with the same magnifying power. Varley likewise delivered the fourth Friday evening lecture at the Institution. This was on the 24th of February 1826, Professor Faraday having delivered the inaugural discourse on the 3rd of the same month.

In 1821 he had married Elizabeth Straker, a cousin of Miss Barnard, afterwards the wife of Professor Faraday. One of the issue of this marriage was Cromwell Fleetwood Varley, F.R.S., the electrician, who had so much to do with the laying of the first Atlantic cable, a man of striking originality, and possessed of not a little of the genius of his father and of his still more gifted uncle, John Varley, of whom he from time to time related to the writer many interesting facts and anecdotes. Singular to relate, Cromwell Varley was a confirmed spiritualist; and the way he became one was this. There was much talk about the "phenomena" of spiritualism and the "manifestations" to be seen at spiritualist circles. Believing these to be all sheer trickery and humbug, he thought that the application of a little of the scientific method to which he had all his life been trained would speedily result in a thorough exposure of "the whole rag-tag and bobtail of conjurors and quacks," as he put it himself, "who were imposing upon and making capital out of the credulous public." He was so sure of being able to show up the whole system of trickery and fraud practised by the mediums, that he designed to write a pamphlet on the subject for the enlightenment of the world. But when he went to work to apply his scientific tests, he found the matter not so easy as he thought. In short, he was speedily made aware that he had got into deeper water than he had imagined, and, instead of exposing spiritualism, became a convert thereto.

But to return to Cornelius Varley: in 1822 he accepted the appointment of governor of some mines in Brazil, a very lucrative appointment, and everything was arranged for the voyage; but on his discovering that slaves were to be employed on the estates he at once threw up the engagement, an act thoroughly characteristic of the man, and illustrative of the intense aversion he had all through life to every kind of tyranny, whether physical or moral.

In 1850 Mr. Varley was elected chairman of the committee of exhibitors in Class 10 of the Great Exhibition of 1851, and received a prize medal from the jurors for his Graphic Telescope forty years after its introduction. He was the author of papers, among others, on the following subjects: Atmospheric Electricity, communicated to the *Philosophical Magazine;* Improvements in Lathes for cutting Screws, for polishing Lenses, and in the Manufacture of Iron and Steel; on Live Boxes for Animalculæ; Cages for keeping Plants and Animals alive for several Days to watch their Progress and Development; and on a Phial Microscope for the continuous observation of *Chara vulgaris* and *Nitella*. These latter, with other microscopic observations, were communicated to the Society of Arts, and are published in their *Transactions;* while a series of microscopic observations extending over thirty years, communicated to the Royal Microscopic Society, were published in the journals of that Society. He was likewise the author of *A Treatise on Optical Drawing Instruments*, and he published a series of *Etchings of Boats and other Craft on the River Thames*. The last-named was the only work amongst the many he wrote dealing directly with the subject of art to which he put his name.

As an artist Cornelius Varley did not come near his more celebrated brother. His works were few, and for the most part of a semi-classical and somewhat conventional character, introducing architecture and groups of figures. They were composed with care and generally finished with much elaboration. There was a quality in his work, however, which always gained for him the respect of his brother-artists.

Among his chief works exhibited at the Water Colour Society were, in 1809, "A Mountain Pastoral"; 1810, "The Sleeping Shepherd"; 1811, "Evening" and "Palemon and Lavinia"; and 1815, View at Ardfert, Ireland. In 1816 he exhibited "Evening in Wales"; in 1819, "Ruins of Troy"; 1820, "The Vale of Tempe." In the following year he resigned his membership of the Society.

For forty years he formed one of a small sketching club, which met at the houses of members, and comprised such men as J. M. W. Turner, R.A., J. J. Chalon, R.A., A. E. Chalon, R.A., H. P. Bone, Josh. Cristall, F. Stevens, and W. M. Sharp.

Cornelius Varley had, while a member of the Water Colour Society, occasionally sent a work to the Academy exhibition; later he exhibited his principal pictures there, though seldom more than one at a time. He exhibited for the last time in 1859.

At his death he was the oldest member of the Society of Arts and the last survivor of the founders of the Water Colour Society.

John Linnell, who knew Cornelius Varley as well as he did his more famous brother, speaks of him as having been of a more religious turn than John. He was by profession a Baptist, and it was through his inducement that Linnell himself went to hear the preaching of the Rev. John Martin, a well-known Baptist of that day, and in the end became a member of his church. But while he makes this statement about Cornelius, he confesses that he had not the courage to follow his convictions to their logical or legitimate conclusion, as he himself did.

Where Cornelius had the advantage over his brother was in the methodical habits in which he had been trained by his uncle Samuel, and which served him to good purpose all through his life. Hence he was enabled to make the most of his smaller abilities, and to keep clear of financial difficulties which his brother, with a far greater income, was doomed to struggle with all his days, and finally had to succumb to. Treatises have been written to establish the truth of the thesis that genius is near allied to madness. But it would be just as easy to prove that the eccentricities of genius are often to be accounted for by partial idiocy—that is, the lack, or rather inadequacy, of one or more faculty, and the preternatural size or activity of others. In Varley we see the almost total extinction of the power that values money and watches over the pocket, whilst his sense of the beautiful and the faculty that makes a man the perfection of good-nature and geniality were present in the highest degree. Nor does he appear to have had the slightest sense of order or method in his mental equipment, or any idea of foresight or circumspection. His son Albert used to say that when his father was living in Conduit Street, and was in the receipt of an income of something like £3000 a year, he appeared always to be impecunious, and would frequently go to him and borrow small sums of money.

Moreover, connected with his marvellous and indefatigable industry, he displayed a carelessness, and one might almost say a wastefulness, that was astounding. When he had money it frittered away in what others would call extravagances and useless expenditures. For instance, he would have the most expensive articles of furniture made, and when they were obtained, he would think no more of them, but allow them to go to rack and ruin in the most absurd way. Once when he was living in Titchfield Street, Linnell, then his near neighbour, found a costly set of deal drawers, which had been specially constructed for him, full of valuable paper and sketches, under a shed in the yard, exposed to rain, and soiled by fowls, which used it as a roosting-place. Careful John Linnell's sense of order and economy was shocked by such wastefulness. He therefore bought the drawers, removed them to his house, and there had the article cleansed and Varley's paper and sketches put in order.

Surely these facts go in favour of a theory of partial idiocy, rather than in favour of that of the madness of genius. But, notwithstanding all our speculations on this subject, our knowledge in relation to psychology is still in its infancy, and probably will be for a long time to come. When we come to look at the matter in the right light, however, such peculiarities as those displayed in the character of John Varley will be of the utmost value.

All the portraits of Varley that I have been able to discover are two sketches by John Linnell, in one of which (reproduced in my *Life of John Linnell*) he is shown arguing with William Blake; a pencil drawing by William Henry Hunt, in the possession of his grandson; and a lithograph published by Messrs. Vokins, after a drawing by himself. All represent him as a man of marked physical characteristics and of great constitutional vigour; but in Hunt's drawing we see him in a much more refined aspect than in Linnell's vigorous and life-like sketches.

THE END